LOVE
and War
VOLUME TWO

CHARISSE SPIERS

LOVE IS LIKE WAR: EASY TO BEGIN BUT VERY HARD TO STOP.

– H. L. Mencken

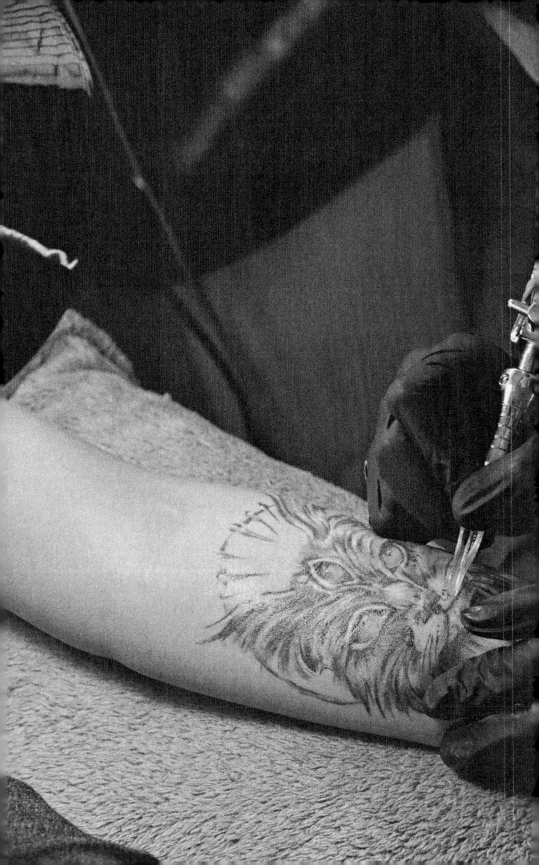

CHAPTER ONE

Kross

I pull back up at the house, body covered in sweat, every muscle aching. I'm pregnant sent every damn childhood memory flooding my mind one after the other like a hit to the head. I couldn't think, I could barely breathe, and the chill running down my spine almost paralyzed me. It was as if reliving them all over again, from the first time the state worker led me to that house to the day I left and never went back. That God forsaken room was there. I could smell the urine filled plastic bottles. I could see the dingy carpet and the messy bed. That spot on the floor I sat day after day staring at the wall, plotting, and wishing like hell I would die came back to me as if I never left. I blacked out, and I'm not one hundred percent sure what all was said from that point forward.

Fear does that to me. My mind forces me to block out everything until I'm able to get my memories under control. Everything becomes physical reflex. My emotions were stunted at a young age. I've only ever been able to work things out internally in the mindset of a child. Normal people learn through experience, feeling, and watching others; through interaction—all things I never had until it was too late.

I spent most of my adolescence locked in a small room, only the necessities at reach, and the only window boarded up from the outside. It was at the back of the house; easily hidden when needed, like to pretend we were a happy fucking family every time a visit from the state occurred.

When everything came back to me I was sitting in the parking lot of the gym, my trainer already waiting from my call when I walked in the door. Who the fuck knows what all I did when I was out of it. After knocking him on his ass during hitting practice I knew I had lost it. I was in a place that's hard to come back from. Usually only one way, and that's almost always when I'm getting rid of a body. Somehow control over a life snaps me out of it. I've never understood why. I park in the garage and sit, trying to calm myself down.

Pregnant.

Fucking Christ.

It can't exist. There is no other way. I know I'm fucked up. It's no secret. Kids need things to avoid becoming like me; things that I can't give. Things that I'll never understand. The world doesn't need any more screwed up kids. That's why I donate so much damn money to help the ones already here, born into this fucked up place— the tormented, the abused, the addicted, the victims. Suicide, drug abuse, sexual abuse, physical abuse, and homeless . . . If there is a fund for it I've donated. That's as far as I can handle. Being active physically and emotionally is impossible for me. I don't understand what people view as good and happy in the world. I only comprehend the bad and the ugly—the pain.

I can barely stomach to be touched by anyone other than Delta, and even that still takes work. I would never damn a child to becoming part of my hell. I have Delta. Delta is enough. She's mine. All mine. In some fucked up way she gets me. She knows when to push and when to stop. She smothers the solitude without forcing me to wade into a sea of people. I can't lose her.

Kids require attention. They're unpredictable. They're hard to control. They change people. She can't change. I have no business being a father. Replicating my DNA is a mistake. I know this. It would barely survive; certainly never thrive. I'm willing to put it out of its misery before it's too late. Before there is no way to back out. Before everything is different, ruined. She'll understand. She always does.

I run my fingers through my hair before finally getting out of the truck, making my way inside. The house is eerily quiet. Every light is off. I search every room, no visible sight of her. Nothing is out of place. Everything is the way it was when I left. I run upstairs. Still nothing. The door to her old room is open, when usually it's closed.

I walk inside and halt. Drawers are cracked open and empty. The closet is bare. Everything else of hers is still here, but her suitcase is missing. I run to my room, pulling open the drawer she keeps a few of her most used things in so that she doesn't have to go upstairs for everything. It too has been cleaned out except for a small piece of paper. I grab it and unfold the two sides.

I choose more.

What the fuck is more? She's gone? But she chose to stay . . .

I don't fucking understand! I grip my hair and pull, a roar

tearing from my chest. My head is spinning. My heart is pounding. My nerves are on edge. I shove over the dresser, slinging everything to the floor. A punch to the wall follows with enough force that my fist surges through it, Sheetrock crumbling. Then I do it again, and again, until a section of the wall resembles Swiss cheese.

I grab the mattress and shove if off the box spring, looking for the handgun I keep between. When my nerves are overworked, taking apart and cleaning guns is the quickest thing to calm them. Resting on top of the solid black piece is a small white square, the center dark. I grab it and turn on the light, the sun already setting. I look it over, trying to figure out what the hell it is. Her name is in the top left corner, other information that makes no sense across the top. The date stands out. Then something she said comes back to me. "I'm eight weeks now. I was six at the ultrasound."

I stare at the middle, my eyes lingering on the small gray center in the midst of blackness. That's it? That's what it looks like? That's our kid? My knees buckle, forcing me to sit. My eyes won't move, but my hand finds my phone and without looking I attempt to call. As it tries to connect against my ear I continue to stare, zoned out enough it doesn't immediately register as the automated message plays in my ear.

"The mobile number you are attempting to reach is currently unavailable. Please try your call again later."

What? I hang up and try again. Same message. I try Kaston. He answers on the second ring. "I figured I'd hear from you."

"Delta there?"

"Yeah, but Kross—"

"I'll be right there."

I disconnect the call before he can finish what he was going to say. I need answers and I need them now.

I barely put the truck in park before jumping out, storming up to the door. I beat on it, not letting up, before finally it opens. It swings open with so much force that I have to re-balance myself to avoid falling forward. Kaston is not the one on the other side. Instead it's a pissed off female. Anger I understand. "Where's Delta?"

"She doesn't want to see you."

"I didn't ask."

"You've done enough."

"Send her out here or I'm coming in."

"Look here, asshole. You may scare a lot of people, but you don't scare me. You come knocking on my door and making demands your ass can go right back to where it came from. She's my friend. I've been in her life a lot longer than you. She's upset. She needs a break. You can see her at work, but not today."

"I'm not in the mood for your shit, Lux. I'm being respectful, but you're inserting yourself into my business. Send her out here."

She stands taller. "No."

I step forward, closing in on her. "Unless you plan on assuming legal and financial responsibility for the thing she's carrying, stay out of it and let me handle my shit," I grit.

Her palm makes contact with my cheek. The tingling skin sends rage shooting through my veins in a way I haven't felt in a long time, and before I can control my feet they move closer, crossing the threshold, my hands clenched into tight fists. Red begins blurring my vision. A hand clenches around my neck and shoves me back. "Outside, Kross. Take a walk," Kaston spits, pulling Lux out of the way. "Get inside, Lux, fuck."

He slams the door, stomping toward me. My vision starts to clear with her out of sight. "Your old lady has a set of balls, Kaston."

"Her temper is about as short as yours. Calm the fuck down," he barks, pointing toward my truck. "Over there, because if you hurt mine we're going to have problems."

I crack my neck side-to-side, my angry eyes locked with his sending a warning my way. The same one I'd be giving if the situation were in reverse. I turn and march to my truck, placing my palms gripped over the side of the bed, leaning over until I'm seething toward the ground. "I'm losing my shit."

"You need to give her space, Kross."

I bang my head against the panel of the truck, trying to make sense of everything. "I need to talk to her. Her shit is gone. It's supposed to be there. I'm used to it being there. I will fucking kill someone, Kaston, and that cocksucker at the strip club is first on my list. You know I will."

"Well, she's here where you know nothing will happen to her. Breathe. Then you can tell me what the fuck you said or did to her to cause her to look like she did when she got here. She hasn't left her room since Lux showed her to the guesthouse out back. She asked me for a job. Delta asked me for a job. It could be just me, but I don't see a girl like Delta wanting to answer phones and do busy work as a career when she is apprenticing under you, unless it's a damn good reason."

My head snaps up. "Like hell she is. Kaston, I swear to God!"

He holds his hands up. "Don't threaten me. What the fuck did you do?"

I run both hands through my hair, frustrated. "I told her to abort it."

"Fuck, Kross, you can't take a woman's options away and expect her to stay."

"A man deserves to know when she's not on birth control. I was nutting blind."

He turns around, leaning his back against my truck. "But you're the asshole that assumes birth control never fails?"

"At least I would have had the option to decide!" He crosses his arms over his chest, seeming at ease and pissing me off more. "What? You should be on my side. What if Lux did that shit? I don't need a kid, Kaston. I wouldn't even know what to do with one. Guys like us don't have families. We're thieves, murderers, and monsters. We're criminals for fuck's sake. We go against moral code. We don't go to birthday parties and parent-teacher conferences. I'm emotionally retarded," I admit aloud for the first time. "I can't connect with people. She told me she loved me and I felt nothing." The stress is wearing on me, becoming too much for me to handle.

He breathes out. "For one, I'd be pretty damn happy if Lux got pregnant. I'm obsessed enough to marry her, why not mark her mine in every way by knocking her up? But it's impossible. She took away my choice before I was in the picture. And who said guys like us don't have families? My dad raised me just fine. I never knew what kind of shit he was doing on the side until I was older. The key is keeping it separate. Just because we do bad shit doesn't mean we'll be bad at parenting."

He turns, propping his forearms on the bed of my truck and looks at me. "Let me ask you something. How many women have you nut inside of, aside from Delta?"

My jaw locks. I look away, every muscle in my arms tense. The revulsion sets in. "Kross, I can't help you—"

"One, and not by choice."

I look back at him, waiting for the fucking question to come that I don't want to hear, let alone answer. He's staring at me. I don't like this whole confession shit. It's not me. Pity pisses me off. "Did wrapping it up or pulling out ever cross your mind when you were with her? Before, during, or after? With Delta. I'm not going to ask you questions about the other. It's none of my fucking business, but if you need a hit I'll gladly take it. On the house . . ."

"It's already done."

"Understood. Moving on."

"No."

"Then I think it's pretty obvious you feel something. I don't know much of your back-story. My dad taught me a long time ago not to go digging in someone's closet without cause, but I've sensed for a while you were dealt a shitty hand. We've known each other a while. I'd like to think we're friends where business isn't concerned. That entitles me to a little personal honesty every once in a while. Just because you don't understand how you feel doesn't mean you feel nothing. We both know if she was nothing you wouldn't be here in a psychotic rage trying to beat down my door."

He pushes off the truck, taking a few steps back. "Love is only obvious if you've experienced it before."

He turns and begins walking toward the house and the panic starts back up again. "I need to see her, Kaston. She's not answering her phone."

He doesn't stop or turn around. "Give her time, Kross. Go home. Get your shit together. The thing you need to decide is do you want both or neither, because she's made it clear it's a package deal."

Home? Alone? I don't want to go home alone. "Kaston!"

"I'll watch her, Kross."

Then he disappears inside. Back at square one. What the fuck am I supposed to do now?

CHAPTER TWO

Kross

I turn for the twentieth time in the last hour. I've counted. Every single time. The whole damn house smells like her. The bed is cold. It's too fucking quiet. The sound of madness. For the first time I can actually hear the slight buzzing of the neon light hanging on the wall.

I grab her pillow and pull it against me, trying to sleep, but I'm wired. All I've managed to do since I got home is shower and stare at the clock. Midnight. Christmas Day. That dreadful holiday to postpone work one more day. Why I promised to stay away till then I'll never know. I had a weak moment. It's the only explanation. I've never followed orders before unless it resulted in a payday.

I was warming up to this bullshit day because of her. It became routine. Every day we came home she plugged in the Christmas tree. There are even a few presents under it she wrapped. Who the hell knows what they are. I don't need or want anything. At least not before now. Now, this day is on my shit list.

I close my eyes, trying to force myself to sleep, to stop thinking. When my eyes remain in a state of nothingness, I open them. It's a wasted effort. I sit up, aggravated, and turn on the bedside lamp. The photo is lying next to my wallet and phone. I pick it up, looking at it again. Shit.

I grab my phone, trying her again. Same fucking recording it's been all day. I toss it back on the table, the heel of my hand pressing against my forehead as I lean over, elbow on my thigh. I can't just fucking sit here.

Then a thought occurs to me. That strip club. A place that exploited her. The guy that was important enough to go back to when she was stubborn and in need of money. Like right the fuck now. The craving sets in. It's already been justified in my mind. I stand, making my way to my closet. Some motherfucker is going to die today, and it's going to be the one she loved first, because he sure as hell isn't going to become an option for last.

Della

The thunder rolls overhead, rain pelting down on the metal roof. It's a soothing melody in a world of chaos. I grab the bag of rice and open it, removing my phone. I can't believe I dropped it in the toilet and didn't even notice till it had been there a while. Thankfully this shit day is over. I try to power it on with no success. I growl, throwing it against the wall. "Piece of shit."

I wonder if he's even upset I'm gone. Or if he's tried to call. I shouldn't think about him. He hurt me. But I can't help it. Since Lux brought me here to this small guesthouse with a bedroom, bathroom, central space, and small kitchen, I've just wanted to be alone. What more could I possibly need here?

A large body, covered in ink, decorated with scars, wrapped around you while you sleep . . .

"No! That's not what I need." I glance around, hoping Lux didn't walk in. I'm only going to look crazy talking out to no one. Kross doesn't want our baby. I've had a lot of time to think, sleep, and miss him. Too much time. And I don't even have my phone to occupy my mind. It's a recipe for disaster.

The front door opens and closes. Lux walks in, flipping down the hood on her raincoat. She holds up a thermal insulated carrying bag. "I brought you food. You need to eat."

"I'll probably just throw it up. You can put it in the refrigerator for later. Why are you awake at this time?"

Her shoulders rise and fall with her breath of desperation. She removes her coat. She's offered me food twice already today. I've yet to eat any of it. I don't have the appetite for it anymore. She makes her way to the small kitchen and sets the bag down on the counter, unzipping it. She removes a crockpot and plugs it in. "Soup. It's broth based. Helps with queasiness. Not an excuse this time." Then she pulls out a sleeve of saltine crackers. "I've amended the menu to accommodate first trimester pregnancy."

The tears begin to fall again. I've tried to push the baby to the back of my mind in an effort to not allow resentment to build. It doesn't deserve it. It didn't ask to be created. She sets the crackers down and rushes toward me, pulling me into a hug. "Delta, please stop crying."

The blubbering begins, my tears soaking her shoulder. "I

miss him—his silence, his moodiness, his demands. I miss it all. I've thought about this all day. You don't know him like I do. Occasionally he gives me pieces of himself —the guy that he keeps buried for protection. He has a tormented, beautiful soul, and I've only scratched its surface. Some of the times that I sat and thought about this pregnancy I wish I could do it. I wish I could turn off the fact that I already love it, that I care, and I think that with one act I could go back and be us again, but then the guilt consumes me for even having those thoughts when your angel is in heaven. What kind of person entertains the idea of getting rid of her child?"

"A girl that's heartbroken, Delta. It's okay to be upset. Had I been old enough to really understand what was happening to me I likely would have been too."

"Before today I had some hope that he would accept it. I expected anger, even fear, but I still hoped he would want it. That we would be a happy family in the end. We created life. That's a beautiful thing, whether it was on purpose or not. I feel like two different people inside. Part happy and part sad. It's making me crazy."

She runs her hand down my long hair. "He came by today. Well, technically it was yesterday."

I lift my head. "What? What do you mean came, as in past tense. Where did he go?"

She breathes deeply. "Sit down, Delta."

"Where did he go, Lux?" I ask, my heartbreak quickly turning into agitation.

"Delta, sit down," she commands in a harsher voice.

I storm over to the couch, sitting down. She follows me. "You were upset and hurt. He was angry. You told me you didn't want to see anyone."

"That didn't include the father of my child! Especially after he stormed out of the house with looks to kill."

"Exactly why you needed a break. He wasn't in a good mindset. I told him he couldn't see you. "

I stand. "You didn't have that right! You should have come and gotten me."

"He said things. I slapped him. You weren't in a place to deal with that kind of shit, Delta. If you were you wouldn't have left."

"You don't understand him. It's obvious. I need to make sure he's okay. He says hurtful things sometimes. He doesn't mean them like any other guy would. He reacts without thinking. That's a result of his background. All he's ever known is negativity, solitude, and abuse. I've dealt with it just fine and never slapped him! Oh my god."

I begin to pace between the coffee table and the couch. "If you don't care how he treats you then why are you here? Why did you leave if you're just going to give in to his every controlling demand?"

"I left because it was the only other choice without obeying him. That doesn't mean I don't still love him, Lux. Just because I chose to keep our baby against his wishes doesn't mean I want to completely abandon him, to cut him out. I'm giving him what he wants—a life with no kids. I can't even hate him. And I've imagined how hard it's going to be to do this alone. He's had enough people in his life do that. He's a direct result of hatred and pain. He doesn't intend to be cruel. It's reflex. Some would even call it mimicking. What's sad is that it's not hard to see if you just look. He may be a dick a lot of times, but you can also be a glorified bitch when you want to be. If you would take off your own judgmental blinders you would see you're a lot like him, and Kaston loves you anyway."

"Okay, okay. Truce? Please sit down. Let's talk this out. You know I only want what's best for you. I always have."

I do as asked, falling back against the couch. My hand finds the tattoo on the back of my neck, rubbing along the place his name is written in permanent ink. "If there were ever a moment I knew without a shadow of doubt he loved me, that he wanted this, even after everything he said, I'd go back. But until then, I'm giving him what he asked for. I'm showing him a life without us in it. I have to stand strong. I have to protect our baby. Because once it's here, I have to know one hundred percent that it'll always feel wanted, unlike me.

She sits back to match my position and grabs my hand, kissing the back of my fingers. "For the record, you're the strongest girl I know."

We sit in silence, listening to the rain on the roof. We're in a torrential downpour and all I can think about is Kross, wondering what he's doing, if he's okay. Then, without effort, I pray.

God,

I know I'm probably the last person that deserves a wish. I've done things in my life that I'm not proud of. But, if you have a little extra grace to spare, please bring him back to me. Please make us a family.

Amen.

CHAPTER THREE

Kross

I glance at the clock on the radio display. 4AM. I've been sitting here for the past two hours, off the driveway between some pine trees, ensuring no one else shows up. I holster my knife in my boot and my gun behind my back in the waistband of my jeans. It's time. It's been too fucking long.

I've had plenty of time since I followed him here to locate every flood light on the front of the house, to check surroundings, and to work my adrenaline up.

I make my way to the house along the tree line, out of sight from the security light. One dim light remains lit up inside the house. It has been since I arrived. I check the sliding glass door. It's unlocked. I ease it back slowly and quietly walk in, looking around. Two wine glasses sit on top of the counter with barely any liquid remaining inside, one wearing a pair of red lips around the rim.

Giggling commences. "Chuck," a female voice says in a flirty way.

One step at a time I move through the main area of the house, in front of the mantle. I stop, my eyes being pulled toward the picture frame sitting on top. My jaw locks into place. Long black hair. Tattoos I recognize. She's younger, standing in a parking lot, hands laced on top of her head and staring off as if she's dazed. It's a candid shot coming from an angle most often used by stalkers and private investigators. Everything is the same except her eyes. The ones I'm familiar with look alive. These remind me of the ones that walked in the shop that day to drop off her design for her tattoo: lost, sad, void.

My eyes move to the next. There she is again, but this time she's in lingerie and heels, sending my rage into dangerous depths. Innocence is ingrained in every feature all over her face. Insecurity of a juvenile girl is in the way she holds herself without clothing. She's too fucking young to be dressed like that. One by one my eyes study them. He's got photos of her all over the room. *Of my girl.*

Then a female moan sounds, and all I can fucking picture is Delta. Lying there under him. Him touching her. Putting his mouth on her. Mine. She's mine. His house is like a fucking shrine of her. He's not over her. Then I hear my worst nightmare. "Just like that, Delta." A grunt sounds. "You always were so tight." Everything goes red, blurred, and I swiftly move toward the continuous sounds, some feminine, some masculine. "You like that, baby? Tell me you love me."

The words are returned, high-pitched. I walk in the bedroom to a girl with long, black hair bent over the bed, taking it like a fucking animal in heat. He's thrusting into her, calling her by a name that doesn't belong to him. And I fucking lose it. My fist becomes a vise around his neck and I shove him against the wall, the blade of my knife already out and pressing against his lips.

I look back at the girl that's now staring at me, scared. *It's not her . . .*

"How old are you?"

"Fif-fif-fifteen."

"You always let men get off to your body while they pretend you're someone else?"

She stares at me, saying nothing, a look of innocence and embarrassment on her face. It all comes flooding back. Every fucking time I was forced to lay there while she fucked me, while she sucked me, while she milked me. She tormented me mentally, physically. She repulsed me, but she still made me hard. She made me touch her. I hated her. And the last time, I fucking killed her.

I breathe heavily, my nails digging into his skin, gagging sounds occurring. "Get the fuck out of here. You better forget you were here or I'll come after you too."

She grabs her clothes and takes off running, only seconds occurring before the door slams shut. My eyes bore into his until recognition hits. "It's you," he chokes out against the flat side of the blade. I clamp my hand harder, teeth clenched, drawing a gasp. "Delta."

His face is turning blue. I loosen my hold, not ready for him to die yet. That's too easy. Too peaceful. I lightly run the blade along his cheek "You're fucking little girls."

He tries to jerk out of my hold and I slam him against the wall. His hand goes to my wrist, trying to push it away. I tighten my hold again. "Age means nothing to girls like that. They know exactly what they're doing. They seduce men like us. They want us to want them. Look at how they dress, the makeup they wear, and the way they act."

He has a baby face. A headful of thick hair he keeps a little on the shaggy side. Looks younger than he is. He was probably a playboy in school that didn't amount to much of anything. I press the tip of the knife into his skin; drawing a bead of blood. I feel the release as the skin separates, and then I slowly slice down his pretty-boy face. He likely uses it for bait, using sex with young girls as a fountain of youth. With each centimeter I cut through a little more anger leaves me. He growls. "What do you want from me?"

"What was Delta? She one of your kid fucks too?"

"The worst kind. She's a fantasy, a sweetheart, an addiction, and an obsession. Those green eyes lure you in. That body hooks you. The sadness she hides makes her an easy target. A little attention and she was riding my cock better than any other girl ever has. That little vixen is still the best fuck I've had."

I'm counting his pulse. Watching his heartbeat. If I don't I'm going to snap his neck. And that's no fun. "But you already know, don't you? Or you wouldn't be here. She love and leave you too? Word of advice . . . Move on. The bitch is needy. Makes a good cock choke. That's about it."

"So you can have her? Not a fucking chance." I knee him in the balls once and then the dick before shifting him around in front of me so that he's facing the mirror, neck in the crook of my arm, his naked ass against me. He coughs, his hand going for his dick, trying to hunch over, but I hold him straight. "I hope I broke it," I seethe. I turn my knife around toward him; handle up. "Take it. You know you want to."

He stares at me. "What's with the black latex gloves?"

"Take it," I demand.

He grabs the black handle. "Who the fuck are you?"

"Your worst nightmare. And I'm about to rid the world of mine."

I shove the needle into his skin, injecting the PCP. He tries to strike me with the knife and misses, my gun already aimed at his temple. "Okay, Man. What do you want? You can have it. Just let me go."

"First, I want to know why you have so many photos of her. Since she's just a cock choke and all."

"Because she's mine. Always has been. When she's done with her little phase she'll come back. She already was till you got in the way. The second she started moaning against my lips and choking my cock with that still-tight pussy after all these years, I realized nothing had changed. I put in the time. She knows who wants her, who will take care of her. Your kind is just a fantasy for her—the tattoos, the muscle, the attitude—something that won't last. When she's done playing with you she'll come back. Always does. Another pussy didn't even take her away from me."

The anger dies down, burning out like a flame, and all that remains is indifference—the point in which I know I'm gone. There's no turning back, even if I wanted to. *If . . .*

I don't.

"That's where you're wrong, motherfucker. She's mine. The way I see it—only way to solve this is for one of us to die, and it isn't going to be me. Blade to the gut. Let's go."

"What? No."

He tries to struggle, but I tighten my hold, shoving the barrel of the gun into his skull. "You can do it or I can, but if I do it, I won't stop until I'm wearing your blood. It's your choice."

His hand starts shaking. He holds the blade toward his abdomen, three inches from the skin. "Please. Let me go. I won't touch her. She's all yours."

"See, I don't think that's the case. Then you'll always be in the background. The guy that fucks kids. And well, this is what I think about those people."

I switch my gun to the opposite hand, still holding him in the bend of my elbow. Then, with precise control, I wrap my hand over his over the knife and drive it into his torso. He screams out, hips pushing backward against me in an effort to protect his body. My chest swells. Before her it would be enough of a rush to get hard. Forcefully taking a life satiates something deep and dark that nothing else touches. Every second pulls me deeper. Every blood-curdling cry, every blood-covered tooth spewing droplets as his mouth opens, and every cast-off blood pattern against the floor as the knife backs out to go again channels my mind.

Control drives me.

Thick red flows down his chin like a waterfall. The smell of rust makes me high. Not ready to stop, I pull the knife out and strike again, and again, releasing every bad memory on a stab, and then, as the blood begins to coat my hand and pool on the floor, everything blurs and becomes peaceful. I stare through the mirror, watching every breath become slower than the last. I continue, waiting for the moment that I feel his heart stop and his body become lifeless in my hold.

When there is no sound, no breathing but my own, I release him and he drops to the floor. I squat, taking him in. "Should have never fucked that one. That one was meant for me."

Empty needle on the floor. His handprints on the knife. The door was unlocked. PCP is a hallucinogen. Who the fuck knows what he could have been seeing in his head. Doesn't matter to me. One person that hurt her is gone.

And one of my nightmares will cease.

CHAPTER FOUR

Detta

I grab the door handle and take a deep breath before opening, trying to settle my nerves. I walk in, holding the large box from the donut shop. "I brought donuts. I got them to mix the kinds so there is something for everyone. I already ate mine. Don't judge me."

Cassie looks up from the computer and stands. "Thank God you're here!"

I raise a brow as I set the box down on the counter, suspicious. "Why?"

"Kross came in raising hell. Everything I've done is apparently wrong. He's being an asshole." She stops herself. "Let me rephrase. He's being a much bigger asshole than normal. What's wrong with him?"

I shrug. "No clue. Haven't seen him today."

Her eyes grow wide. "Are you two pissed at each other? Delta, fix him! I've never seen him like this. I cannot deal with this permanently. He's making my dad look like a saint. Fix. Him."

"I can't control Kross any more than I can control the weather."

"Have you been smoking? He's been a much nicer asshole since you started. Again, fix it!"

I turn the box toward her and open it, my nerves only worsening since I walked in. "Sugar solves everything."

She takes the one with sprinkles and grabs a napkin. "Thank you. Now shoo. I've already gotten my ass chewed one too many times today."

Put your big girl panties on and do it.

I grab the box and make my way to the staircase, opening the door. The fact that I hear nothing upstairs puts me on edge. As I step inside the studio, Kross looks up at me from his station, our eyes locking. His hair is disheveled and standing all over his head. He looks like he's been up for at least forty-eight hours. He looks stressed. A ping of guilt occurs.

Stop.

I have nothing to feel guilty about. This is what he wanted. Remington snakes his arm around me and takes the box. "Sweet. I knew I liked you for a reason."

I glance over at him, a smile beginning. "You're welcome. I hope you had a Merry Christmas."

"Remington," Kross says, his voice strained. "Let. Her. Go."

"Why? Trouble in paradise?" he teases, squeezing me into his side tighter.

The boy is stupid. "Hands off. Now."

Remington is still smirking, intentionally prodding at Kross. "I'm just going to remind you of a little conversation about relationship drama in the workplace . . . That goes for you too."

My eyes zone out, mouth slightly agape from shock. I push him off me and slap his arm. "Remington! Shut up. Do you have a death wish?"

"Delta, outside!" he roars, demanding my attention.

"I didn't even do anything!"

He storms through the break room and pushes the back door open with force, causing me to jump. I look at Remington, narrowing my eyes. "I hate you sometimes."

He grins. The fool actually grins. "One of these days you'll thank me." I growl out when he shoves a donut in his mouth, and then dreadfully I trudge across the studio and out the back door.

Kross is standing at the bottom of the stairs, palms on the brick and his head bowed between his arms. He looks up when my feet hit the stairs, and then turns and walks through the small parking lot toward his truck. I follow, climbing in the passenger seat as he shuts the driver's side door. The silence is deafening and the tension is thick, smothering me. "You wanted to speak with me," I finally say.

He's banging his fist against the steering wheel in a steady rhythm. "Your phone. It's off."

I've missed you too . . .

"It's broken. I dropped it in water and it won't come back on. I've tried soaking it in dry rice. It didn't work."

He reaches in the backseat and grabs a white gift bag, filled with red tissue paper, and then places it on my lap. "What's this?"

"Gift."

I tighten my lips together, fighting against the smile trying to form. When everything else changes, Kross stays the same. I love that about him.

24

You're supposed to be angry with him, stupid girl.

I internally sigh. "Kross, I can't take this. I wasn't expecting a present from you."

"You can and will. Open it."

By the look on his face there is no sense in arguing. I pull the paper out of the bag and look inside. I grab the thick rectangular box and pull it out. "An iPhone?"

"I couldn't get you. I'll pay the bill." The smile happens. There was no smothering that one. My little control freak will never die.

"It's not messed up because I didn't pay the bill. I dropped it in water. I was planning on getting another one when I got paid."

"I prefer it this way. My number is already programmed."

I turn toward him, trying to be serious and adult for one damn second. "Kross, you don't owe me anything. We aren't together. I chose to keep it. I'll take care of it. You made your decision and I respect it. It's just not the one I can make."

"We are together."

"No, we're not."

"We are together."

"Kross—"

"We are together, Delta. I never told you to leave."

"You told me to get rid of our baby. That means—"

"I know."

"I didn't obey you. It's okay to want different things, but we can't want different things and be together."

He pulls at his hair. "I'm trying to want the same things."

My heart starts pounding, but my stubborn ways take forefront. "You shouldn't have to try to want the same things. A baby doesn't need to grow up with a parent that feels stuck. Trust me. I know."

He growls. "This is maddening. I want you to come home."

"I can't come home. Did you not just hear what I said?"

"I want you. That should be enough. I'll work on the rest."

My head falls back against the headrest as I die a little inside. I have to stay strong or we'll end up destroying each other. Those with patience win the race. I have to believe it. I want him more than I've wanted anything. I need him more than I need air. "I miss you."

Fuck, boy, stop making this harder . . .

"I miss you too, Kross."

"Come home. I'm going insane."

"I don't know that I can say no to you a second time."

He reaches over the console and scoops me up, pulling me into his lap. "Don't. No is not a word I like to hear. Come home. It's where you belong."

Why are you so easy to love?

My heart is racing. This is more emotion than I've gotten out of him, ever. I just want to make sure he wants me there for the right reasons. "Why? Why do you want me to come back so bad?"

He stares at me. *Just say it. Say you love me.* "I need you."

My shoulders fall. My chest is aching. He's not ready. This baby needs a family; two parents that not only love it but love each other. "How about we take it slow? We can see how it goes. I'm not saying I won't come home, I'm just saying I can't right now. You need time to think, to see if this is really what you want, and not just a reaction because I'm gone. I need stability, Kross. This baby needs stability. I need to know it's long term before I come back. In 'trying', you said you need time to come to terms with the baby, to accept it, to want it. I'm respecting your wishes. I need you to respect mine."

His hand skates up my bare thigh, moving under my skirt, and then his fingers dip beneath my panties. My breathing becomes louder, more erratic with every inch that he gains, until finally he sinks inside of me. "How long you need?"

"As long as it takes." His fingers lazily thrust in and out of me, teasing and tormenting me. "Shit," I whisper.

He pulls my V-neck down, along with my bra, and places his mouth on my nipple. "Still mine."

I grip his hair. "Still yours."

He switches to the other side. "Only mine?"

"Only yours." He flicks his tongue back and forth, forcing me to grind myself against his hand. "Someone's going to see."

"Don't care." His thumb slips between my lips, pressing against my clit. "Tits are bigger again."

My entire body feels like it's on fire, a tingling sensation blowing across my skin. "Fuck me, Kross. Please."

It takes less than thirty seconds and he's pressing into me. My hormones drive me. My body takes the ride. And his hands softly love my body—my breasts, my stomach, and my back. He doesn't force me, but lets me lead. Fast. Hard. Back and forth. The instructions are written in my mind, forcing my body to comply. My lips find his, greedily taking them for myself. He pulls back. "I'm about to come. Without you is hell."

I moan, needing to hear more. "Come in me. You're the only man that ever has."

He bucks his hips upward, driving his pelvis against me. I clamp around him to feel the spasms of his dick as he releases himself inside of me. Without warning I fall into orgasm, releasing all the aches, the pains, and the sadness from my body. Because that's what he does to me. He puts me in a state of chaos, but then leaves me in peace.

CHAPTER FIVE

Kross

The brush sounds behind me. Movement. I remain where I am, sitting on the hillside in a hoodie, the hood flipped up, with my forearms resting on my bent knees, watching her through the windows. She's wearing that pajama set that I like; the white short and tank top set with the small skulls all over the shorts in black. I remember the way it feels. It's soft, the cotton worn, as if it's been washed hundreds of times.

She's sitting on the couch, her back against the arm. Luckily she's sitting on the right side so that I can see her face. Her long hair falls over her shoulder as she looks at her new phone. I glance down at mine, staring at the pinpoint on the aerial map where her phone is located, checking for accuracy.

A person takes my flank. "You going to sit on my property all night?"

My eyes return to her. "I figured you'd notice me at some point."

He offers me a bottle of water. "What are you doing here, Kross?"

"Respecting her wishes."

"Here. Hydrate. You've been out here since nightfall."

I decline. "Don't need it. Won't even know I'm here. I just need to see her."

"Take it. You look like shit. Are you sleeping?"

"Did a line of blow. I'm good for a while."

It's silent for a moment. The way I like it. The wind blows, the leaves of the trees rustling. "You're tracking her? You don't think that's a little much?"

"Never claimed to be normal."

"I told you I'd watch her. Do you not trust me? After all this time . . ."

"I don't trust anyone with her. Nothing personal."

She stands, walking toward the bedroom. I move my head around, trying to get her back in view, but within a few seconds she's back, pulling on a long-sleeved shirt. My shirt. The last one I wore before she left. She pulls the collar to her nose, holding it there. "When it's not a hit it feels like an invasion of privacy. Can't you just track her from home?"

"I'm good here. She won't come home. Her smell is there, some of her things; it's not warm anymore. Nightmares are back. When she left they returned. It's not the same sleeping alone."

"She'll come back."

"I killed him."

"Who?"

"The fucker from the strip club. The one that had her first. The one that had Delta stripping. The kid fucker. She was fifteen. Like me. Just a kid. Confused about life probably. He was grown. He knew better. She looked a lot like Delta without the tattoos or the piercings. He even called her Delta. I went on a psychotic whim, pissed she was gone and worried she'd go there, but then he had pictures of her everywhere. Nudes, lingerie, candid shots, posed shoots. She was younger. A lot younger. Some I found before, some after. I snapped. My girl was all over that fucking house. I injected him full of PCP and forced him to gut himself. I need to be here, Kaston. If she won't come home I'll come here. I swear I won't tell her or try to go in. I just need to see her."

"Stay as long as you want. I get it. I was disposing of the body of Lux's ex not all that long ago. Rich fucker. Someone will miss him." He places a hand on my shoulder and then he stands, leaving me in peace. I didn't even flinch that he touched me. Not sure what that means. I either completely trust him or am more fucked up over her than I thought.

She turns on her side and curls up, placing her hand over her stomach, protecting the baby I'm not happy about. The thing that caused all of my distress.

That girl fucking like a woman was someone's daughter. Parents probably didn't even know where she was. Probably didn't care. People bring kids into this world and feed them to wolves. That could have been my daughter. Spreading her legs for a grown man. I'm psycho enough. I can't handle the thought of a kid. But I can't stomach the thought of losing her. The only person that's ever understood me. Cared. Loved me. *Loved me.* I have to learn to want it. A kid can't take her away from me.

She yawns, and then turns on her back so that she can use her phone with both hands. My phone lights up, a text coming through.

Delta: WYD?

Me: Nothing.

Delta: Thank you for the phone.

Me: It was for my own selfish reasons.

Delta: I want this to work.

Me: Me too.

She doesn't immediately say anything.

Me: Come home.

Delta: I will. When it's time.

Me: You're driving me crazy.

Me: Literally.

Delta: You're being dramatic. You've probably barely noticed I'm gone.

Me: I've noticed.

Delta: Maybe we could do something tomorrow? After work?

Me: Ok.

Delta: I think I'm going to go to bed. I'm tired. Goodnight, Kross.

Me: Goodnight, Delta.

Delta: Kross.

Me: Delta.

Delta: I love you. You don't have to say it back. Or feel like you should. I wouldn't want you to say something you don't mean. I just want you to know that I do.

My thumbs hover over the keyboard, reading the words over and over. I glance at her. She's doing the same. I finally find the words.

Me: I'm starting to believe you.

Delta: As long as you do, the rest I can live with.

Me: Get some sleep. You have work tomorrow. None of that working with Kaston bullshit. You've already left me once.

Delta: :(I didn't leave you. Okay I did. But to be fair I thought it was my only option. Don't ever think I've left you. I'm only giving you space.

Me: Sleep.

She gets up from the couch and walks to the bedroom, turning off the overhead light, only leaving on the table lamp. She's beautiful. I'd give anything to go back to sleeping next to her. I'll change my whole goddamned life for her apparently.

CHAPTER SIX

Delta

"Babe," Lux says, opening the office door as she knocks. "Can we come in?"

Kaston looks up from a stack of papers on his desk, a cup of coffee to his right. It's early. It was my only chance to talk to him before I had to leave for work. He looks so . . . I don't know, domestic. Like a professional. And he's not even wearing the suit I've seen him in a few times. I need to stop being so stereotypical of what criminals are supposed to act like, look like. He does have a legitimate job.

Focus.

I came to the house early in hopes he'd see me. Something has been bothering me. Call it my motherly intuition kicking in, but it's taken the forefront of my mind to the point that it's making me crazy. He waves us in. "He works from home on the days I don't have school," Lux says, rolling her eyes in a way you know is utter love and not annoyance. "So there is no rush."

I follow Lux to the guest seating facing his desk. We sit at the same time. She crosses her legs and places her hands in her lap, as if we have an official appointment. How formal of her. My hands are connected in my lap, my insides knotting together. He looks at me, and then her, his brow rising; then a smirk sets deep in his face. "Ladies, to what do I owe the pleasure?"

You have to do this. It's for our family.

"Well, it's funny that you asked. Delta has something she needs to ask you."

He glances at me. "What you got for me?"

I inhale and breathe out. "I was wondering if I could ask you for a really big favor. I know that the two of you have been kind enough to let me stay here —"

"Delta," Lux whines.

I hold up my hand to stop her. "It's a kindness I am not owed. It means a lot to me. I know the two of you are trying to start your lives together and need your alone time, so I'm grateful that you're giving me a place to stay and I have no place to ask for a favor, but it's not so much for me as it is for someone else."

Kaston places his elbow on the arm of the chair, his forefinger rubbing his upper lip, studying me. "This about Kross?"

"Yes."

"Continue."

I try to calm my nerves, hoping that if this goes through Kross doesn't get pissed at me. This isn't something to take lightly. If this doesn't end in my favor, it could be the end of us, but I need this closure. "I would like to hire you to find out about Kross' birth mother. He doesn't remember her. He thinks he was abandoned.

He was left to rot in that hellhole with a woman that tormented and abused him. I'm still shocked she was a foster parent with the kinds of things she did to him, and that no one ever noticed! For the life of me I can't imagine how anyone could raise their child to a certain point and then just leave him. I want to talk to her. To find out why she did it. There has to be a reason he was sent to live in that hell. I need to know."

He leans forward, placing his forearms on the desk with his hands clasped together. "So let me get this straight. You want me to dig up Kross' past without his permission? Also my dealer. The person that I use for very specific, illegal needs. Finding an arms dealer is not like contracting out for plumbing or electrical. There is trust involved. There is risk. And you want me to blow that trust to shit and back for something that doesn't benefit you or me? I don't think so. There's too much at stake, and I'd like to think that he's more than just a business contact. I don't fuck over my friends."

I release the breath I've been holding, disappointed, and nod. "Okay, I understand. Thank you for letting me ask at least."

I stand to leave, but Lux grabs my hand, pulling me back down. "Now wait one damn second. I love you, and I understand your point of view, however, if I remember correctly you dug up my shit without my permission!"

"You only know that because I told you. I had my reasons."

She narrows her eyes at him. "And she has hers!"

"Lux, it's fine. Please don't get angry over my stuff. My intention was not to cause any problems between the two of you."

"No, Delta. It's not fine. Kaston, she's pregnant with his baby. His baby! He's the father of her unborn child. That opens him up for personal things. It's no longer just business. You know if I wanted you to dig up shit on Sophie's dad you wouldn't even hesitate."

"There is a difference in a sperm donor and a father."

"You don't even know him. Do you really want to go there? Staying on topic, Kross is having a hard time dealing with it. Did it ever occur to you that maybe it's because he had a rough childhood . . . like me? She keeps saying we're similar, well, then I'm going to speak for him as if walking in his shoes. Maybe if she got some answers it would be closure for him too. Everyone needs closure! We all have shitty moms, even you. You looked her up when we were still new. That brings us all together in ways. You want to make me happy? This would make me happy. Not a fancy wedding. Or a honeymoon in the Cape. Although it may surprise you, family trumps all of those things. She's my family, and she's hurting. This is something she needs and you have the resources to give it to her. She never asks for a damn thing."

I want to curl away, the awkwardness settling in. Kaston looks at her in a way that seems so private. They aren't speaking. Then finally he breaks, the tension in his body leaving, and he's suddenly sitting relaxed, before looking over at me. His voice softens. "What makes you think he wants to know if he's never looked into it himself? I'm almost positive Kross has his own resources for information."

"I don't think the demons have left him alone long enough for him to consider it. He's haunted, Kaston. You have no idea."

He rubs his hands up and down his face and leans back in his chair. "I need to think about it. There are two people I've considered off limits when it comes to deep digging: Chevy and Kross. Their information, aside from a standard background check employers use, is private and I've respected those boundaries to keep it that way."

"That's all I'm asking," I say, my heart quickly pushing its way to my throat.

He opens a drawer and then lays a notepad in front of me with a pen. "List any information you know, should I decide to look into it."

I stare at the lines covering the paper, before closing my eyes. *I'm doing this for you, baby. Both of you.*

Then, I pick up the pen and call upon any information I've filed away from conversations we've had; stories he's told. Within minutes the tip of the pen begins to move.

-Possible name: Rachel Brannon.

-State of residence: Illinois.

-All counties within a-hundred-mile radius of Chicago.

I think, pen shaking. *Those fucking neon lights. The stage he recalled from a kid's point of view. The dancing. His reaction to me stripping.*

-Background information: possible stripper. Maybe even prostitution.

-Transferred to foster care young. Approximately twenty-six years ago.

-Biological father: Unknown.

The details of that story comes back to mind. I didn't get memories out of Kross often, but the times he gave me clues or information of things inside his head I made sure to memorize them. I'm not sure about this, or any of it for that matter, but I'm going to go with my gut instincts on this one. Something about his name and the way he remembers that particular detail sends chills down my spine.

-Biological father: Could possibly be the club owner. Large cross tattoo covering full side of neck.

I cap the pen and slide it back to him. He glances over the details, and then places the notepad in the same drawer he got it out of. "I'll think it over. If I go against my better judgment and decide to dig, I'll let you know after the fact. There is no reason to get your hopes up if I find nothing."

I nod, gathering my purse to leave. But before my butt comes off the chair something overwhelms me. "Thank you, Kaston. I know it doesn't seem like it, but I really just want what's best for him. I love him more than he'll ever understand. Deep down, further than anyone could imagine, I believe he's just that scared little kid that was left with no answers, no memories, and was thrown from family to family until he got stuck in the worst one of them all. Where we had freedom he knew captivity. When we had choices he was practically a slave. We know a shitty, lonely childhood and he knows pain and solitary confinement. He had no guidance, only torment. When Lux and I had each other to get through our issues he had no one. We walked away and he sacrificed to leave. Of course he's cruel, controlling, and hard. It's the result of everything he's been through. His only way to cope is to block out everything that normal people thrive on. This baby, the one thing that makes so many people happy, scares him to death. Fear drives anger. Even if it doesn't work out with him and me, I need to know what kind of person would do that to her own flesh and blood. It's the only way he'll ever know peace, to ever forgive, to ever learn to love."

I stand and walk to the door, grabbing the doorknob. "Delta."

I turn at the sound of Kaston's voice. "If you feel that way and he's pursuing you then why haven't you gone back?"

"Because I'm giving him the one thing he was never given before: options. And I'm making sure our baby never goes through what we did: parents that don't want it. When I know he wants us both, and loves me, then I'll run back to him and never leave again. I need to know it's more than his need for control."

And with that I walk out the door, my nerves relaxing the second I am on the other side. This has to work. I need to find that little boy and show him that he's loved, and always has been.

I get in my car and toss my purse in the passenger seat, before sliding the key into the ignition. I sip my white chocolate mocha and place the coffee cup in my cup holder and the bag holding my ham, egg, and cheese bagel on the seat. I turn the key over only to hear the stall of the engine. I stop and try again. Same thing. "No . . . No. Please don't do this to me."

I get out and lift the hood, checking underneath it for God knows what. I have no idea what I'm looking for. But I do check that the battery cables aren't corroded like last time this happened. They still look clean from having to replace the connector.

I walk back to my car and try to crank it again. Nothing. I slam my hands against the steering wheel over and over, before tears spill from my eyes. "Why do you fucking hate me? I don't need this today."

My head falls against the headrest. "He's going to be pissed at me for being late."

I glance at my phone. 7:52. Me and Remington are on schedule for the same time today. I quickly find his contact and call him, putting the phone to my ear. He answers after only a few rings.

"Delta? Are you okay? You've never called me. I wasn't even sure why you wanted my number."

"Are you at work yet? Please say no."

"No. Just left to head that way. What's up?"

"Will you come get me? Please. My car won't crank."

"And Kross?"

"Had an early appointment. I don't want to make this situation worse by pulling him away. I figured you were closer than my friend."

"Where are you at?"

"Java Drip."

"Okay, I'll be there in ten."

"Thanks, Remington."

"Uh huh. You just remember who's your friend when he wants to beat my ass."

"Oh, don't be dramatic. It's a ride. Last time you provoked him."

"See ya in a few."

I disconnect the call and wait. Might as well go ahead and eat. Because it's probably going to be hell on wheels when I clock in late. Kross' easiest pulled trigger.

Kross

I place the bandage over the triceps tattoo and roll back on my stool, tossing my gloves on the tray. "Good to go, Man. Keep it moist. No soap or scrubbing until it heals. Touch ups for new tattoos are first Tuesday after your appointment from three to five if you've lost any color. Cassie will get you downstairs."

"Thanks. Appreciate it," he says, tapping the bottom of his fist on the top of mine. He walks toward the door, just as I glance at the clock. 8:10. She's fucking late. The one thing I do not tolerate is tardiness. It makes or breaks a company, especially when someone else can't just fill in with your client on a tattoo. It looks bad on me more than anyone if I put up with it. She doesn't get special privileges. I fight the urge to track her, to assume the worst. Kaston wouldn't hire her out from under me. He wouldn't piss me off that way.

Then it dawns on me. I look at the schedule. "Where the fuck is Remington? And Delta?"

The tattoo guns stop. The two girls getting matching shoulder pieces by Joey and Wesson are staring at me, wide-eyed and still. "Uh, Boss," Joey says, nodding toward one of the clients.

"Where are they?" My voice booms across the room. "One of you better know why they are both late."

He glances at Wesson, and Wesson shrugs. "Kross," Cassie says over the intercom.

I press my finger over the button, trying to control my temper. "What?"

"Can you close the ticket for Jake so I know what to charge him?"

Shit. "Yeah. Give me a second."

I stand and walk to the employee computer, pulling up the appointment information. I put in the charge and close it out. Every feeling racking my body proves I need to go outside and take a break before I do something I'm going to regret. Footsteps sound on the back stairs.

I force open the door, halting Delta in the center of the stairway, Remington close behind. She glances at me. Only a second later her eyes dilate and she says. "It's not what you think."

Usually when someone says that shit that's exactly what it means. "Then enlighten me, because this doesn't look good."

That urge is coming back. Now that I gave in, it's coming back even easier. And the one standing behind her is the one I want. "Fuck," he says. "I told you."

"Let Remington go inside and we'll talk. He did nothing wrong."

"He showed up late with my fucking girl and I don't see your car. Based on the fact that you aren't winded it's not likely that you walked. I'd say that's a pretty good reason for someone to die today."

"Kross," she growls. "I called him to give me a ride! My car wouldn't crank."

"I don't recall my phone ringing."

"You had an appointment. I have the schedule memorized just like you told me to. There was no reason to pull you away when Remington was on his way."

I stare at Remington as I hand her my keys. He stands tall, crossing his arms over his chest. "Go get in the truck."

"Nooooo! Not until you let him go inside."

"Delta, for the love of God, go get in the fucking truck!"

She flinches. "Delta, it's fine. I can handle his shit. Just go," Remington says.

She glances between us—me at the top, him at the bottom, before looking back at me with tears in her eyes. "He's my friend. They were all my friends, especially Wesson in the beginning, before us. He's the only one that doesn't act scared of you in spite of being my friend, unlike the other two in there that have made things fucking awkward when you're around. Just because someone has a dick doesn't mean I want it. After all this time you should trust me."

Then she walks off, stomping her feet the entire way to my truck.

I internally sigh, fighting a smile. I descend, one step at a time, until I'm standing face to face with Remington. "What's wrong with her car?"

His eyes scan mine, and his stance relaxes from the defensive one it's in. "I don't know. I told her to lock it and you could check it out later."

"I appreciate you not leaving her stranded, but next time you better fucking call me first. Are we clear?"

He smirks. "Sure thing, Boss."

"Congratulations on not being a pussy. You just made manager. Now go run the shop until I get back. We'll go over details later."

And with that I walk off, appreciating the sound of his feet running up the stairs. I need men with backbones. Not pushovers. The only ones that can earn my trust are the ones that can take my shit and handle it. I have a lot of business that goes on behind the scenes of my shops, and I sure as fuck don't need someone that will break under a little pressure. There is a method to my madness. A good king knows how to build his kingdom, starting with his soldiers.

Detta

I stare out the window, remaining silent. I'm angry, sad, and a little embarrassed. I'm angry that he would jump to a conclusion such as that one just because I asked for help. I'm sad that having friends is so hard. And I'm embarrassed that Remington was right the entire time. "You going to be pissy the entire ride?"

I glance at Kross as we continue down the highway, his comment sparking my temper. I stare at him, dumbfounded. "Why wouldn't I be? You basically accused me of cheating on you! With a coworker!"

"You should have called. You know the rules about being late, Delta, just like everyone else."

"My car wouldn't start! I handled it in the quickest way I knew how. When are you going to give me some fucking credit instead of finding shit in every damn thing I do? You want me to be at work on time. I call Remington to eliminate more time instead of calling Cassie, having her get you because you don't pull out your cell gloved, and making you leave when you're in the middle of working. In the midst of all this I ate my breakfast so I didn't throw up everywhere. I did not have time to call you! We take one step forward and two steps back, Kross. Fuck. It's exhausting."

I take a deep breath, my eyes pouring tears once again. "My car wouldn't start," I repeat.

He glances between the road and me. "We're about to deal with your car. Why are you so emotional?"

I start crying harder, and then without stopping begin laughing manically, my face wet to the point my eye makeup is smudging. "Oh, I don't know! Maybe because I'm pregnant and my hormones are all over the damn place and I love you so fucking much but you make me absolutely crazy. I'm losing my damn mind."

I close my eyes, trying to get a grip. My fingers become laced with his warm ones, catching me off guard. My eyes pop open, honing in on our connected hands over the center console. Instantly I calm. "It's making you weird."

"Yeah . . . I guess growing a human will do that to you." I stare at our hands; shocked he's holding mine. "Do you really think I'd cheat on you?"

His hand clenches around the steering wheel. "Trust doesn't

come easy for me. And you're not home. I'm used to you being with me all the time." He pauses, and for a moment I think he's done. "I'm trying, Delta, in the only way I know how."

My heart breaks, and the guilt flows through my veins freely, reminding me of everything I had temporarily forgotten. I shouldn't have gone off on him like that. "I would never let someone inside of me when I'm carrying your child, even if we weren't together. And I definitely wouldn't cheat on you." He's staring straight ahead. "Kross." He glances at me. "I would never cheat on you. At some point you have to trust me until I give you a reason not to."

He turns back to the road, and then he squeezes my hand. My heart mimics the action. I glance back out the window. It suddenly dawns on me. "Where are we going? We're nowhere near the coffee shop."

"Dealing with the car situation."

My brows furrow. "Are we going to a parts house? I don't understand."

He pulls into an Infinity dealership. "No. You've been driving that piece of shit long enough. I'm done."

He stops off to the side of the lot and throws the truck into park, shutting off the engine. I look around at all of the shiny, brand new vehicles sitting side by side in rows, all different shapes and colors. The words manage to come out just in time to hit the lock button as his hand goes to pull the door handle. "You are not buying me a car!" I start breathing hard. "I can do this on my own. I can deal with car trouble. We just need to figure out what part it needs."

My hand starts shaking, hovering over the lock button in case he tries to open the door again. I won't be my mom. I won't expect a man to support me while I play with my money. He closes his eyes, and then shakes his head. He looks at me with a smirk on his face.

"What's so funny?"

"You done?"

"This isn't a joke, Kross. I've been saving my paychecks aside from food and my cell phone bill. Now, thanks to you, I don't even have that. Just figure out the part and I'll buy it."

"Why are you so against having help?"

"Because I won't be that girl. That girl—"

"Like Lux?"

"I didn't say that."

"But you were thinking it."

"No. Don't put words in my mouth. Lux has her reasons. She was upfront with Kaston. She never lied about her initial intentions. I have my reasons for wanting to do it myself. I can support myself."

"I'm no expert on being a couple, but what I keep hearing is self. We're either together or not. I already told you we're together. You agreed. I thought you wanted me to want this baby."

I rear back, trying not to overreact. "I want you to want it if you want to want it."

He pulls at his hair. "Delta, stop being so fucking complicated. This pregnancy wasn't planned. Quit acting like I'm a dick because I'm not overly happy about it. Just because it takes time to want something we didn't try for doesn't mean I never will. This is me starting to want it, because I want you. Your car broke down. It was long overdue. We both knew that rusted piece of shit wasn't going to last much longer. My kid isn't riding around in something that can crumble upon impact like someone crushing a coke can. That thing is unsafe. I've never wanted you in it either, but now I have a reason to get my way. You want me to trust you, then give me the same respect. I knocked you up. There is no reason to do it alone. I can take care of you and my kid, because next time you may not be lucky enough to be parked in a public parking lot during daylight. Let it go."

My shoulders fall. I feel defeated. Every point he made makes sense, as much as I don't want to admit it. I said I was going to put this baby first and that means in every way. I look around again. "Why Infinity? I don't have to have something this expensive."

"You remember that conversation we had in Chicago where I said I'm not hurting for money?"

"That doesn't mean it has to be unnecessarily spent."

"If you're going to bitch every time I spend money on you then it's going to last a fucking while. And that guy walking over here . . ."

I glance up, and sure enough there is a guy covered in neck tattoos wearing a baby blue button down and khakis walking over. He hasn't even looked away from me, so I have no idea how he knew he was coming over. "I help those that help me."

"Help you, as in . . ."

"Yes."

"Do you have *people* everywhere?"

"Yes. Just because we're having a baby doesn't mean that's going to change. We amend."

"I've never asked you to change, Kross."

"Then get your fine ass out of this truck, introduce yourself, and go pick out a damn car, because I have a full day of clients and we aren't leaving here without one."

"But."

"Out."

I growl, internally happy and frustrated at the same time as I open the door, letting one leg fall over the seat. "Are you not coming too?"

He glances at a phone I don't recognize. "After I make a call."

I step to the ground and face him. "Will you at least tell me the budget?"

He taps the keys on the old school flip phone, not looking at me. "Whatever the price is on the sticker of the one you choose. I'll deal with the rest later. Give me five minutes. It's business."

I dramatically slam the door, before waltzing in front of the truck to meet the dangerous looking guy waiting a few feet away as if he knew to wait on Kross before getting too close. I scream when he blows the horn at me, my heart speeding up. And when I give him my best 'go to Hell' look he smiles. God, I love that stubborn man, even when he drives me nuts.

Kross

I pull into the back parking lot of the shop and park behind the new black Infinity Q50 two hours later, with only fifteen minutes to spare before my next appointment arrives. I've carried the phone around trying to decide on the job. Today, finally, I made the decision to decline. Truth is, I have too much shit going on in my life right now to take that kind of risk and use that much time. I need my girl back. I want her home. I have to come to terms with the fact that I'm going to be someone's father, whether I want it or not. It's the only thing I can't control if I want her.

I've never turned down a job when we're talking millions of dollars being wired to an offshore account, but for the first time something is more important than money. She's more important. So when she got out back at the dealership I made the call. I turned it down and gave him a contact for another dealer.

I place the cell phone and the folder with the details of the job in the manila envelope and seal it, writing the name of the pickup on the front so that I can drop it later. I get out, locking up behind me, and walk to the driver's side door. Three taps to the glass with the knuckle of my forefinger after a few seconds of standing here. She lets the window down, her hand clenched at two o'clock around the steering wheel.

Her head slowly turns until her flushed face is looking at me. I bend over to her height, leaning on my forearms on the door. "Fuck, that was so much fun."

I pull my bottom lip between my teeth, trying not to laugh. Her light blinds my darkness on days like today. "Fun huh? So I guess you're over being pissy about me buying you a car then?"

She pushes her lips out into a kissing position, and then breathes out. "I'm still not happy about how much it cost, but there were a lot worse price tags on that lot that I stayed away from. And I'll admit, it's hard to be mad when you go from driving the ole punch bug to this fine metal specimen."

"Punch bug?"

"Ya know what? Never mind. This thing even has Bluetooth!"

I laugh. "Aren't we years past being excited over that invention?"

"Not when you've never had it in your car before!"

Her excitement is contagious. I reach in and touch her face, running my thumb over her smooth cheek. "I like seeing you happy."

She grips my wrist softly, closing her eyes under my touch. "It's you, Kross. You're the difference."

When she opens her eyes they're brighter, a mischievous gleam in them. She brushes her hand up my arm until it's holding onto the back of my neck, pulling my head inside the car. "Can we christen the back seat?"

My dick hardens. "You want to fuck in the backseat of a car? Like two teenagers?"

She smirks. "You bet your ass I do."

"My client will be here in like ten minutes."

"I can do it in five," she says, her voice changing, causing my dick to strain against my jeans. She pulls me closer, before swiping her bottom lip over both of mine. "Come on, baby. I'm wet."

I grunt. Damn. I straighten and move to the back door, then open it and stuff myself in the small back seat. These cars weren't made for big men. I don't know how in the hell this is supposed to work. My knees are shoved into the back of the seats and my head is pressing against the headliner. Uncomfortable. This is fucking uncomfortable.

The window slowly ascends, leaving us on the other side of the tint. She presses a few buttons on the radio until the local rock station is playing. Her eyes meet mine through the rearview mirror. They're different than normal: confident, seductive, and happy. Fucking sexy is what she is when she's like this. That's for damn sure.

Then, without a word, she gets out of the front and walks to the back, glancing around as if she's trying not to get caught doing something wrong. She quickly opens the door and jumps in, shutting us inside. Before I can process she's removing her winter boots and pushing her jeans down her legs, disposing of them on the floorboard.

She looks up at me, pushing the last of her pants off her feet, a smirk on her face. All I can focus on is a bare pelvis, the top crease introducing what's waiting for me the second she spreads her legs. "What you waiting for, baby? Let me see the D."

God, she's fucking beautiful. I robotically unbuckle my jeans and push them down, baring my lap. Her eyes fall on my erection and the quietest moan slips, making me harder, also motivating her. She straddles me, her lips instantly finding mine in a heated entanglement.

I push her sweater up her body and remove it. "I want to see tits," I mumble against her lips as I remove her bra. My lips trail down her chest until they find a nipple, sucking the ring into my mouth. She arches against me, and then grinds her pussy on me. A hand grips each ass cheek as her wet center rubs against my length, holding her firm.

A thud sounds as I attempt to move my foot. "I can't move."

She kisses me. "Don't worry, baby. I got you."

That smirk. Why the smirk? Then she turns around, facing toward the windshield. "Someone is going to see your tits. Those are my tits."

She grabs my dick in her hand and aligns it for entry. "I don't even care right now," she says through shortened breaths, and then she sits down on top of me, her tight pussy gripping me the entire way. She pumps. Up and down. Up and down. Hot and wet. Shit. I roughly grip her ass, opening her to watch as she takes me inside her.

She's holding onto the headrests, speeding up and moaning so loud it's making my dick jerk inside of her. Her spine rounds, her shoulder blades moving as she rides me. I've never fucking known anything like her. I grip her ponytail holder and pull her hair down, her black hair falling over her back. She speeds up. My palm anchors on her stomach. She slows on an intake of breath, and then she lays her hand over mine and laces our fingers.

I pull her back against my front, my free hand harshly squeezing her breast. She rocks against me; the pace no longer bursts of quick aggression. She breathes heavily, rocking harder as she finds the target. I thrust up at the moment she comes. Her head falls back against my shoulder as she rides out her orgasm. Seconds after she's done she increases speed until she's pumping up and down on my dick so fast I can no longer last, spilling my load inside of her.

Spent, I press my lips on the top of her shoulder. She turns her head toward me, her lips at my ear. "I love you, Kross."

I freeze. Hearing her say it, not overhearing it, or reading it, is so much more profound. I wrap my other arm around her, my palm still pressed against her flat belly, and pull her closer. "If I knew what that felt like, Delta, I can guarantee I'd love you too."

She pulls off of me and turns around, gripping my face in her hands, tears in her eyes. "We're gonna make it. I know we are."

I breathe in, and breathe out, and for the second time in the last five minutes I let the thought in my head out. "I hope you're right, because I'm fucking miserable with you gone."

CHAPTER SEVEN

Kross

Love is greater than any aspect of the mind. Love is an oath, an action, and a constant choice to surrender oneself to another.

I stare at the words on her left ribcage as the needle injects the last of the black ink. I've had some crazy requests; some love confessions, others marriage proposals, and then there are the memorials. The list goes on and on. As a tattoo artist I see it all. Nothing surprises me anymore. The human race is crazy over the thought of the whole love thing. It's a greeting card holiday three hundred and sixty-five fucking days a year. I've done a lot of tattoos, and more script than I can remember, but never in all the years of me inking human skin has one got me to thinking.

Thinking that it's a truth instead of an observation or opinion. It's the first time in my entire life that something in regards to 'love' makes sense. The concept of love to someone that's endured hatred for a lifetime is bullshit. It's a made up notion to market products: jewelry, flowers, candy, and products in every fucking category. The list is never-ending.

But looking at it in terms of a verb versus a noun makes all the difference. It makes sense. It becomes something I can understand. Feelings are something I don't. I'm numb. I'm emotionless. I don't believe in sparks and magic and whatever other fucking ludicrous behavior is associated between two people. The only realistic human behaviors are lust, desire, need, obsession, jealousy, and hatred. It's easy to see. Look around.

A choice.

Choices I believe in. We all face them. There are always right and wrong ones. Consequences of each. Choices can be taken or given. They can be negative or positive. They can be life altering or have no affect at all. They can be permanent or temporary. They often come after any of the above actions.

I glance at her—Delta.

She's sitting at the extra station drawing; something she does often when the studio is clean and all the artists are busy. I've made many choices when it comes to her, most out of character for me. I desired her so I chose to employ her. I wanted her so I chose to have her. My obsession with her led me to keep her. And my need for her will ensure I never let her go. I'm addicted to what we have. My jealousy will never spare a life when it comes to her. No human, big or small, will take her from me. I'm psycho enough to mean the words.

An oath to surrender oneself to another. That's easy. I don't want anyone but her. If I did I wouldn't be entertaining the idea of fatherhood. Consistency is something I've always needed, just never in terms of a female . . . until her. I don't know what the fuck it is about her that has had me from the start. I'd like to pretend it's the tattoos, the piercings, but in my world that's a common denominator.

No, it's just . . . her.

Do I love her? Sounds impossible. Ridiculous even. What do I know about loving someone? The boy no one wanted. I'm bound to fuck it up if I try. The one thing she expects from me is that I'm constant. If I suddenly become unpredictable that could lead to disaster. Wanting her to the point of obsession is good enough. I will have her. Only me.

I wipe the words again with the wet paper towel and give her the small mirror to look at the finished product. "There you go."

Her eyes change as she reads it over. "It's perfect," she whispers, reverently. I nod, and then rub ointment along the lines before covering it.

"Keep it moisturized to avoid as much peeling as possible."

She flips her blonde dreads from one side to another as she sits up. "Thanks, but I'm pretty sure I've got the instructions down by now. Been working on my sleeve over a year." She smiles.

As I've learned to say to the know-it-alls, "It's like the fucking Miranda rights. If you don't say them your ass will regret it."

"No doubt," she says, holding out her hand. "Just figured I'd give you a break from being a broken record. I get tired of saying it too. She holds out her hand. "Name is Chyna. Just moved here from Phoenix."

"Chyna?"

"Like the wrestler, yes. My parents had a sense of humor."

"Chyna." I shake her hand, before turning toward the eyes burning into my neck. Delta is no longer drawing. Instead, she's staring at the girl as if she's waiting to see if she needs to put a bullet between her eyes. Makes me fuckin' proud. "We can save the introductions. Your tat is done."

Her smile grows. "You're one of those, huh?"

"I'm not sure I care enough to know what one of those are."

"Not interested in anything but a job. Like I said, I just moved here. Need a new gig. Thought I'd feel out the local talent, see who's hiring. I was starting to think the asshole owner of this place was sexist till I saw the cute girl playing with her pencils. Trainee I'm guessing."

"I'm the asshole owner. Not hiring."

"Mind if I leave my resume and portfolio? No harm in that for later, right? You know, just in case something happens to come open."

"Do what you must."

She glances back at Delta, giving her a wave with that same smile on her face. Delta quickly diverts her eyes back to her sketchpad. She turns back to me, not making a move to get off my fucking table. "Unless there is something else—"

"She know you feel that way?"

"What?"

"I saw you eying the tattoo."

"I can't tattoo it without 'eying' it."

She smirks. "I think I'd like working here."

"Like I said, not hiring."

"So, does she know how you feel about her? That she's the one?"

I'm getting annoyed with her questions, but if it'll get her out of my damn shop . . . "You're trespassing onto private territory. What makes you think she is?"

"Just a vibe. I'm pretty good at reading people."

She pauses.

"If that were true you wouldn't still be sitting here."

"You haven't told her you love her, have you? I can see that you do."

The bitch is still talking, and obviously can't take a hint. "We're done here."

She hops off the table. Finally. "You should get on that. Tomorrow isn't something we're entitled to; it's something we're given. Time with someone is a gift. Just as fast as someone walks into our life they can leave it. Don't take it for granted. I'll see my way out."

She walks through the studio, glancing at Delta on her way out. Without so much as a look my way Delta jumps up and runs after her, leaving her pad on the chair. *What the fuck?*

I stand and rip off my gloves, before walking toward the chair, grabbing her pad. It's a skull—half dark, half light. The eye socket of the dark is light and vice versa. The two fade into each other perfectly, reminding me of a yin and yang symbol, except the light half is filled with flowers, making it feminine to the masculine counterpart. Beneath it reads:

Together, we'll always find balance.

My jaw steels, trying to understand the weird-as-fuck sensation in my chest. What I do know is I want this on my body, and she's going to do it. Good thing it's test day . . .

Delta

I open the cabinet and look inside. immediately closing it. Under the chair comes next, and then the empty drawer. "Where is it?" I whisper, searching high and low for something I've been working on for days. I swear I left it here when I went to talk to that Chyna girl. She made Kross uncomfortable; that makes her important. And I caught the small detail of 'portfolio', meaning I could finally meet a female artist, so I set my jealousy aside and I was out the door before she made it halfway down the steps.

After I claimed my break to talk to her and get her number, Cassie had a family emergency and had to leave, so I got stuck working the front desk. It didn't stop long enough for me to return to the studio until now, when the last customer is long gone.

"Looking for this?" Kross asks, tossing something down on his chair as he emerges from the break room. The sound of weighted paper hitting against a hard surface has me turning toward him. It's similar to a flapping sound. It's my sketchpad.

"How long have you had that?" I ask defensively. "That's personal, and I've been going crazy looking for it." My sketches are private. They're usually a result of what I'm feeling or a mood. My sketchpads are like an artistic diary for me. I try to only sketch impersonal things at the shop, because the boys have a tendency to look over my shoulder no matter where I sit or what I say. But since we had sex in the backseat of my new car and I got a small glimpse of real emotion from him and the roundabout way of him saying he loves me, I couldn't help it. My feelings were overwhelming me and I had to let some of it out. With Kross the messages between the lines are the most important of them all.

"Since you ran downstairs after that nut job."

He doesn't even look sorry that he took something of mine, regardless of whether I carelessly left it on the chair or not. That's supposed to be my station; at least until he fills it with someone else. "That's a hateful thing to say. She is nice. I like her."

"She's a meddler. I don't like her."

"Why, because she actually tried to have an open conversation with you in regards to our relationship? At least she acknowledges that we are in one." I smile, halfheartedly joking when I say, "That's more than I can say about a certain someone. The only time you claim me publicly is if we're out of the state or you think someone is hitting on me."

His face hardens. "I'm your boss."

"You're also my boyfriend. I'm not saying you have to grope me in public, but the occasional touch or kiss or even hug would be nice. Everyone knows we're together, so why do you still hide it?"

"You work for me." My head falls back. He said the same thing in the opposite way. I don't know why I'm bringing this up, but the fact that Chyna noticed and asked and he couldn't admit to anything got me thinking. "I have to maintain professionalism."

I breathe out, agitated, and before I can shut my damn mouth the words fly out. "Then maybe I should apprentice somewhere else so we can try to create boundaries. I don't want to be a secret. At some point I'm going to start showing. If you want to keep work and personal lives separate that's fine. Remington told me the artist that mentored him is willing to take me on. He has a small shop across town."

Then his entire demeanor changes to something dark and scary, sending chills down my spine. His eyes . . . He looks like a fucking demon. "He did, did he," he grits out, and then without another word he swipes my sketchpad and storms across the studio, heading for the door to the lobby. It hits me that Remington is downstairs watching training videos in Kross' office.

Oh, fuck. What have I done?

I take off running and block the door with my small body, willing to be a martyr if that's what it takes. It was simply a conversation between Remington and me when I first left Kross. I was grasping at straws to continue learning when I thought Kross and I were done. "Move, Delta," he spits.

"Kross, leave him alone. It was a conversation when I thought we were over. Do you really think I would have kept working here if you had wanted our baby and me out of your life? Come on. I had to think of options without you. He was being a friend."

"I'm going to fucking kill him. He's minded my business one too many times. His body is more useful as gator food than to me. Move out of the way or I'll move you myself."

I don't doubt for a second he would, so I think fast, and that consists of launching myself onto his body and climbing him like a bear would a tree. His hands go to the door to brace himself from the weight change; one in a fist holding my pad still. "Kross, leave him alone," I say in the strongest voice I can muster.

His chest is heaving, his neck corded with full blood vessels, his eyes locked with mine. "No one fucks with me and walks away alive."

"It was a suggestion. I wasn't mad. It's not a horrible idea. I would miss you, but I don't want to push you with too much too fast. You have your rules for a reason. You need certain things and I need certain things. It was a plausible solution for both."

"The fuck it is!" he roars. "You already left home. You sure as fuck are not leaving the shop too. This is the only place I get to see you. I swear to Christ, Delta, I will kill everyone in my path. I already took care of that little girl molester Chuck the fuck."

Every ounce of color drains from my face. I can feel it. My face is cold. My heart starts pounding against my chest so hard I can barely catch my breath. I squeeze my legs around him tighter. My nails dig into the back of his neck. "What did you do?"

"What needed to be done," he says, not an ounce of hesitation in his voice.

"Kross," I whisper, closing my eyes, tears stinging behind my lids. "What did you do to him?"

When I open them he finally says, "I stopped his beating heart." The coldness in his words are scary. It's an unmistakable change by the stagnant air around us. I'm in love with a natural born killer. Lux explained Kaston. He's different. He has some morale behind what he does. It's not right, but it's understandable. He's okay with killing bad people, but Kross, Kross is another thing entirely. He kills with no need for justification, and I don't know very much of what he's done.

"Oh, God," I say, the nausea setting in. "We are going to have a child, Kross! What if you get caught? I'd be left alone while you rot in jail. I don't want to be the reason someone dies!"

He pushes my back against the door, his palm going to my thigh. "When are you going to learn that I don't get caught? I'm a sick fuck. One thing I had plenty of growing up was time to think, to plot. I decide how I'm going to do it before it's done. Everything is calculated, precise, and clean. I'll slit my own fucking throat before I go to jail. You should think about that next time you throw some bullshit out there about training under someone else. No life is too valuable, except yours."

My heart melts. God, I love him. Wait, what the fuck am I thinking? "He didn't deserve to die! Why would you kill him, Kross? I can't even believe we're having this conversation!" I whisper-scream. "He hasn't messed with me since I walked out of the strip club!"

Panic is running rampant throughout my body. I feel like I'm in the twilight zone. "Shouldn't have left; although, what fucking universe are you living in? He was fucking you in high school as a grown-ass man. He was fucking your sorry excuse of a mother when he wasn't fucking you. He was feeding off your immaturity, your weaknesses. He did the same when you went to him for a job. He guilted you into fucking him by using it as bait when you asked. I may be messed up, but I've never manipulated you. You didn't see me forcing you to fuck me for the job. I sure as hell wasn't giving him the option to do it again. I may have gone in there in anger, but then his house was a fucking shrine of you. My girl. All over that fucking place. Photos, videos, panties in Ziploc bags with shit written on it—all of you. I had to see my goddamn girl spread wide for another man while I cleaned that place out. You know what he was doing when I got there? You want to take up for him then I'll tell you. He was fucking a fifteen-year-old girl that was a close replica of you; even called her by your name. I have zero tolerance for adults that fuck teenagers. Just because they're old enough to understand what's going on and mentally take it as if they want it, doesn't mean they actually do. I thoroughly enjoyed watching him gut himself like a fish. Nothing made me happier than seeing his eyes haze over. And if I could I'd go back and watch it all again."

I stare at him, all of my nerves completely burnt out from what I just heard. It's like being the girl to the serial killer in a horror movie. I'm unsure of what to think, how to react, what to say. Still, even after hearing it all, I love him. I can't imagine the thought of being without him. But something doesn't make sense. "Did you say videos? I never made videos."

"I guess the knight in shining armor you gave your virginity to wasn't as charming as you thought. Had at least a dozen of them. I'd say he had a hidden camera somewhere in that house back then. I ever find out they were sold I'll hunt them all down, killing the owners one by one."

My eyes well up as the nausea rises from my stomach. I feel so stupid. Embarrassed to no end. I can't even look him in his eyes. "Where are they now?"

"Destroyed."

I nod, and suddenly something occurs to me that never has before. The tears finally fall as I stare at his body in my hold. "I don't want it to be like us," I admit. "I want its life to be different. I don't want it to suffer."

To my surprise, his palm rubs along my cheek, pushing my hair back. "Delta," he says, his voice quieter, his tone softer. I glance up at him. "I may not can promise you a lot of things, but one thing I can is had that been our daughter, I would have sawed his limbs from his body one at a time, no pain killers, dragging out his death. I will protect the two of you."

My heart skips a beat. He acknowledged our baby. I trail my hand around the side of his neck, along the cross scar that he still hasn't explained. But now isn't the time. I lean in, but before I can kiss him he pulls back. When I look over he's holding the pad not far from his head, my latest sketch on the page exactly as I left it. "This us?"

I feel so bare. I've thought about that symbol since Lux and I talked about it. In ways it fits her and I, but more so, it explains Kross and I perfectly. "Yes."

"What's it mean?"

"I'll be the light to your dark, you the dark to my light. We may be contrasts of each other, but we're the perfect complement."

He forces me off of him and walks away without allowing me to try and kiss him again. My body slumps against the door as he quickly puts more distance between us. Skin. I see skin as he pulls his long sleeve shirt up his body and steps over his chair, removing it. Déjà vu sets in. "You coming or you going to stand there all night?"

He sits, as if nothing previously happened. No crazy talk about committing murder or killing sprees. No, he just sits down and places his shirt balled up behind his head. I want to lick my way around his body. Touch is the greatest sensory we have. And with him I'll never get enough. "Coming where? What are you doing?"

"It's test day. You're going to put that on my ribs, beneath my heart."

My eyes widen, my nerves trying to run away. "No. I can't. It was nerve wracking enough tattooing your body with an outline and a small design. There is no way I can tattoo that freehand. Kross, I'm not ready," I spew in a panic.

He opens his station drawer and grabs his matte black Beats by Dr. Dre Studio3 Wireless Headphones and pulls them over his head until they're wrapped around the back of his neck. He fishes out his phone. I've noticed he wears them when he has long, multi-hour sessions with intricate artwork. Every time I'm hella jealous too, because they're expensive, something I'll never be able to afford. "Go do the transfer," he says, holding out the sketchpad, looking down at his phone as he touches his thumb to random locations on the screen.

I grab my pad. "Did you not hear me? I'm not ready to tattoo you, Kross. I almost died of a heart attack and anxiety the last time, and all I did was outline it. And you want to wear my drawing? A very personal drawing at that. This isn't like Chicago where I just put something I thought was cool on your back with a marker. I . . . I need to make sure it's perfect first. Just . . . not yet."

He sets the phone in his lap and grabs each earphone in his

hands, pulling them over his ears, but doesn't release them to form a seal. "Go, Delta. You can tattoo practice skin all day every day, but you're never going to be ready if you don't try. That spot needs to be filled. You practice every night before bed. You're ready," he says, and then releases his hold on the earphones and lies back once more before closing his eyes, using his shirt as a pillow; telling me this conversation is over without words.

I look down at the drawing again. He wants my symbolism of us on his body . . . under his heart. Forever. That has to mean something. That has to mean love. Why else would anyone want something so permanent?

Kross

The heavy beat of the metal music blasts through my ears as the needle pierces my skin in rapid succession, creating a constant grating feeling. My mind blankets my skin with a numbness I only feel under a tattoo gun. It's one reason I love getting tattooed.

I peek through closed eyes, as I have done the entire time she's been working. Her onyx hair is folded into a high ponytail holder on top of her head, falling forward a little in a fanned out manner from the hunched over position she's in. I've come to like her hair like that, because it doesn't hide her face, and when she turns around I'm rewarded with the sight of her neck tattoo that I did and my name amongst the ink, forever on her body.

The feel of her skin on mine creates a calming effect I've never been able to understand. My anger recedes and I'm left with peace; something I rarely find. Her left glove-covered hand is spread wide over my sternum, supporting her weight as she holds the vibrating gun in her right. She only moves it every so many seconds to grab the paper towel under it and wipe the excess ink away.

I've tried to stay in my head, eyes closed, in an effort to take away her anxiety. But she doesn't realize how much more desirable she is like this. She's focused, in deep concentration on the task at hand, and letting her movements become second nature. She's holding the gun like it's a part of her. And fuck if she isn't sexy.

With each practice session at the house she's proven she's ready. She's driven and it shows. When I wasn't teaching she was doing, alone. I never had to make her practice. The truth is I miss her late night practice sessions. I miss the sound of the buzzing when I would walk downstairs because she was nowhere to be found. I miss the way she looked when she was lost in her head as her hands obeyed her mind's command. When she cursed on a mess up. And when she gleamed at a piece she was proud of.

I would stand there and watch her until she realized I was there, just wondering how in the hell I ended up with her. How something so perfect walked into my shop. And more, how someone so beautiful inside wanted an asshole like me. I know I'm a hard guy to be around. I live under a constant dark cloud, full of doom and gloom. Moody as fuck. It's the only way I know how to be. And she tries so hard to love me. The only girl I've ever had an interest in, aside from the occasional fuck just to prove to myself that sex did appeal to me.

That became our norm. We were lost in our own world and I want it back. I gotta have it back. I stare at her, no longer peeking, remembering how good it felt to sleep with her every night, and counting every second it takes her to do this tattoo, because once it's done she'll go back to that fucking guest house while I sit on the hillside like a stalker and guard her all night—my irreplaceable inked masterpiece.

This is what she's meant to do, who she's meant to be. Her confidence is what needs work. And because of her hard work she'll be rewarded. To the point that I have a Christmas present for her that's going to come on New Year's Eve. I did actually get her a Christmas present. I completely fucked up Christmas, I know this, but better late than never.

There will always be learning in this world, and it takes years to gain the knowledge that any of my artists have under their belt already. Artistry is an industry to never be perfected and is ever changing. Even replicated, no two pieces will ever be the same. There will always be better processes, new skills, and different techniques to learn, and it is not humanly possible to fully teach someone in months' time, so she'll have to remain under the title of an apprentice for at least a year, but because of her drive I'm going to open a new process at *Inked aKross the Skin*. I don't think I've ever been excited about anything in my entire life, but I can't wait to see the look on her face when I tell her what it is. It's something I would have never even considered before her.

Two hours, thirty-eight minutes and forty-five seconds she's been at it. And she finally turns the gun off and sets it down. She cleans the worksite, the skin red and sensitive, before she takes a deep breath, staring at it while I stare at her.

I pull my headphones off my ears and leave them hanging around my neck. She's still staring at the tattoo. "It's finished," she whispers, unsure of herself. She rolls backward, grabbing the handheld mirror off the small counter and holds it up toward me. She's shaking. I grab her hand around the handle to steady it, and then look into the reflection.

My eyes fixate on the details, scanning every spot. The damn sketch didn't even do it justice compared to this. Somehow, out of all the tattoos on my body, I think it's my favorite. No, I know it's my favorite.

"Kross," she whispers. "Please say something. Just tell me if you hate it. I can take it. I'm ready for the criticism. What should I have done different, better? Remington should have done this one. He would have made it look like a professional instead of an amateur's work."

I pull on her hand, and in turn the mirror as well, until she's coming off the stool and toward me. I jerk her onto my lap, forcing her to straddle me. The mirror falls from her hand to the ground, causing a thud and a fracture in the glass. I don't even care.

Her hands find my chest, mine grip her thighs, and she leans forward. "I wouldn't change a damn thing."

"Are you just saying that because we're . . ."

"Have I ever spared your feelings in the past?"

She shakes her head. Her green eyes scan my brown ones, and when I don't say anything else she smiles. White teeth, thin lips, narrowed eyes. I've learned this is her happy. And to a guy like me her blinding smile scorches a darkened soul. She makes me wish I knew how to love someone. Because if I did I would love her in the way that she deserves. "Tell me what you're thinking. Please."

My hands glide up her body until they're pressed against her face. "Now you have a part of me, and I have a part of you. Forever. It can never be erased."

"I like the sound of that," she whispers, and then she presses her soft lips against mine, and like she always does, she worships me. With her mind, her body, and her soul.

CHAPTER EIGHT

Kross

I stand at the door and knock three times. Waiting. I hate fucking waiting. If she would come back home I wouldn't have to. Kaston answers, dressed casual in a pair of jeans and a long sleeved shirt. I'm still not used to the no suit thing he's had going on for a while now. "Kross," he smiles, holding out his hand. "To what do I owe the pleasure?"

I raise a brow, still staring at the hand I've rarely shaken. It's an oddity to me and one I only do on occasion and by force. "How long has it been? You're becoming too normal. I don't like it. Go kill something. We clicked for a reason."

He laughs and leans into the doorframe, crossing his arms over his chest. "I was 'normal' when we met, years ago in Spain. The only things I knew back then were hot girls, fast cars, and private school. My father was the mass murderer, in case you have forgotten with his passing. Did you also forget that at one time I was a detective and not an assassin? We were not on the same sides of the law, my friend."

"Yeah, but I knew back then you had it in you. Why else would anyone want to learn the law from front to back coming from a family of killers? You know you like it too much to quit. You don't just up and decide to be an honorable, law-abiding citizen. Tell me, how does Lux like this newfound family man?"

He rubs his stubble. "She'll get used to it. She needs stability."

"Or you could just be the man she fell in love with . . ."

His smile returns. "I thought you didn't know anything about love?"

"I don't. Just stating the obvious."

"Oh, I think you're figuring it out just fine. You've had a lot of extra time lately. You have become part of the landscape every night on my security camera. I don't think I'm the only one trying out 'normal'."

"If stalking is normal then I guess so, but I'm just on a short break if you're referring to business. Things need to get back in order first. Something of mine is missing. Speaking of, where's Delta? I need to see her. I have plans. Don't give me shit. At least I came to the front door and knocked."

"And here I was thinking you were here to take me up on that double date offer . . . I'm going to assume from the extra estrogen I have in and out of my house that you chose to close for New Year's Eve and Day?"

"Might as well. Then I don't have to listen to my bitching artists complain about not getting good spots for the countdown throughout the city. Business is good enough it won't affect anything. And not a fucking chance. From the looks of you we wouldn't like the same kinds of dates."

He goes for his back pocket and pulls out tickets, fanning them out to show the four in his hand for a New Year's Eve event located in one of the big hotels in the city. "Good, then the two of you can come with us to this. Lux wants to go out. Open bar. Multiple ballrooms for use. Biggest DJs in the city. Party favors. I booked two rooms so you couldn't say no. I am not going to be the only grown man doing this shit. It sounds a lot like college parties, but these you have to pay for. I shelled out a half a grand for this shit, not including the rooms. I could get drunk a hell of a lot cheaper at home and chase my girl around naked if I wanted to, but she wants to dress up and go out. Damn cabin fever or something. Fuck if I know. I wasn't totally listening. She was rambling with her tits hanging out. Lesson of the day: female friends equal mutual interests. It appears we like the same type of dates after all."

I cross my arms over my chest. "I already had plans."

"Not if they include Delta. Lux invited her. She agreed when she knew the tickets were already purchased."

"Dammit, Kaston. How the fuck am I supposed to get her to come back home if we have to tag along with you two? She can't drink. My uncontrollable cock knocked her up in case you have forgotten. She's not going to have fun being around a bunch of drunk people. I had a surprise for her and then I was going to take her to Underground Atlanta to watch the Peach Drop. That seems more our style. At some point I have to learn how to do this relationship shit . . ."

I turn around and take a frustrated breath, looking out across the lawn, my fingers lacing on top of my head. "Because I'm sick of living without her. You started this. It was you that night that planted seeds in my head. I had been ignoring it for months just fine. Now, it's done. She's supposed to be with me. She's going to be with me. I need her. My inner psycho is dangerous with her gone. I can't think straight. My anger is out of control."

"Sounds like love to me . . ."

I turn around. "Is this your way of telling me these feelings don't go away? I'm going to end up with a body problem."

The grin on his face is not amusing. "They don't go away. Tolerable, but they remain." He looks at me, and then his voice changes. "Come to my office. I have something to show you. Then I can give you a plan that will work for us both."

I follow him inside, shutting the door behind me. Her laughter fills the room, coming from upstairs. I hesitate, wanting to go find her, but force myself to continue. Something in his eyes has me curious. And the fact that he has to bring me to his office says it's something I need to see.

I sit in the chair, leaned over. forearms to thighs with the folder open in my hands. With every line I read my anger grows, yet I can't stop. "You did a fucking background check on me?"

He walks around the desk and leans against the wood to my left, facing me. Motherfucker is brave. "Delta came to me. She wanted me to find out about your birth mother."

"And you did it? You went behind my back that easily?"

"No. I told her no. Then, she all but cried and plead her case in that very chair that it was for you. For both of you. Parents to be and all. I told her I'd think about it. I don't pry into the lives of people that are valuable to me. I can tell Chevy has some serious demons, but they're his alone. And unless he betrays me it's not my concern. You were the other one."

I flip the page and stare at my original birth certificate, my jaw locking. "Then why'd you do it? It's no one's fucking business unless I ask for it."

"Because something felt off. I started thinking about it. The way my father refused to use any other dealer. According to the secret books he's poured millions into you. You're in the legit ones too. He invested in your company that's still in the works so that it looks legit. How you suddenly appeared in Spain—an American. So young and already heavy into arms dealing. He had a soft spot for you. I may never know where you came from, but I did some digging in his files back home. Turns out he already knew everything about you. All I had to do was have the files forwarded to me."

I blink repetitively, trying to keep my anger in check. The words on the page are blurred. I don't like being blindsided, especially in regards to my business. "I was a witness."

The words left my lips before I could stop them; a secret so old I had forgotten about it till now. "What?" he asks.

"The men he killed that raped your sister and left her for dead. I watched him kill them. He tracked them, made sure they were nowhere close to home when he did it. It was the first time I ever snuck out, and the last for a while. I was scared when he saw me and took off running. I was just a kid. Years later he found me. Probably to see if I was still keeping my mouth shut. I was already dealing drugs and dabbling in arms. He made me an offer I couldn't refuse. Haven't had problems getting jobs since." The words come out robotically. "No one ever understood me quite like your dad. He taught me things along the way. Had you not killed the fucker that killed him first I would have done it."

"You'll get your chance at revenge," he says. I glance up at him. "Brannon isn't your mother's name, it's your father's."

"My father?"

He nods. I can't even bring myself to read what's in the damn envelope yet. "Just take the folder. I haven't told Delta I'd do it yet. You can tell her what you want or nothing at all. It's your life, Kross. But after reading it, and knowing you, I thought you'd want to know what's in that folder."

I look at the size of the stack held within the two pieces of card-stock. I need to get to Delta. "Summarize. I'll finish it later."

"Your mother was a stripper. Her name was Rachel James. She had priors for prostitution. Had you at eighteen. You were not transferred into state custody until the night of her murder."

I stand, shoving the chair halfway across the room. My head is swarming. I'm dizzy. "Murder? Why wouldn't I have known that?"

"Yes. It's state personnel record; not public knowledge. They found her body in her tiny apartment after the neighbor called the cops for what sounded like domestic violence and a gunshot. You were hiding under the bed, your neck sliced open and screaming for her. It was in a bad part of town known for heavy gang activity. The case went cold. There was no next of kin to take you, so they placed you in the custody of the state of Illinois. Ironically, your mother bounced around in foster care all her life too."

I grip my hair, roar for roar tearing from my throat, trying to stop the pain in my head. Chest heaving, body hot, tingling skin, aggression flowing, I try to calm down with no luck. "What the hell do you mean 'no next of kin' if I have some fucker's last name?"

"Kross, sit down."

"Tell me, Kaston!"

"Sit. The. Fuck. Down. Before you destroy something."

I plop down into the chair, muscles twitching to hit something. "Start talking."

He walks to his desk and pulls out another folder, bringing it to me. "I have no fucking idea how my dad found all of this information, or why he never told you that he had it if he cared enough to get it. He has pages and pages of notes in that folder you're holding. Maybe it's why he created a multimillion-dollar company aside from the illegal activity. He was good at digging, so he charged an ungodly amount to do it."

"Get to the point."

"Your father wasn't listed on the birth certificate. But the owner of the strip club she worked for goes by the name of Elliott Brannon. He has a rap sheet a mile long. There is a paternity test in there to confirm he's your father. He has the tattoo that Delta described of the cross on his neck."

Delta . . . Always remembers the details.

"I'm willing to bet that's where your name came from. He's had strippers come up missing before but there was never any evidence to tie him. The fucker is smart. I'd bet everything I'm worth he's the one that killed her."

"Good, I'm itching to kill something. Someone that sentenced me to Hell sounds like a good target."

I go to stand, but he holds out his hand, stopping me. "There is something you should know."

"The only thing I need to know is where he is and which knife he prefers to have his throat slit with."

"Kross, he's the kingpin of the largest underground prostitution ring to date. Like your tattoo parlors his strip clubs are his legal cover-up. If he were that easy to kill he would probably be dead already. I've talked to a few people. He's like a ghost. This is all I could dig up on him, and it isn't much." I grab the folder out of his hand. "I'm going to assume that cross scar on your neck was a warning to keep quiet. You're not supposed to exist and your mother paid the price."

With the words a sharp pain shoots through my head. I scream out. And it comes back. It all fucking comes back . . .

Someone starts banging on the door. She goes to the little hole in the middle, playing the quiet game. "Mommy?"

She runs toward me on her tiptoes, placing her hand over my mouth. "Open the fucking door, Rachel! I know you're in there."

My heart is beating fast. He's screaming. Still beating. "Shhh, baby. Be quiet for Mommy, okay?"

She jumps when he beats and screams through the door again. "Open the door. If you wanted to keep him a secret from me you should have never come back."

I run behind her as she pulls me toward our bedroom, opening the folding closet doors. "Who is it, Mommy? Are we playing hide and seek?"

"Go in there, Kross," she says, guiding me inside, underneath the clothes. "Don't come out till Mommy comes to get you, okay?"

I nod my head, my cheeks wet. "Am I in trouble?"

She gets on her knees. Tears fall down her face. I don't like seeing Mommy sad. She only gets that way at bedtime. It's not bedtime . . .

Her soft hands touch my cheeks. "No, baby. You did nothing wrong. Mommy is in trouble. I didn't do something my boss told me to, but you did nothing wrong. Do you understand?"

"Okay. Why are you sad?"

The front door flies open. Heavy footsteps begin to sound in the other room. "I love you, Kross. Remember, Mommy loves you. Always have, always will."

As soon as she closes the doors, leaving me in only darkness with stripes of light, she's yanked backward by her hair and she screams. My heart leaps forward, but I stay still like she said. I get prizes if I mind. And I don't want to make her sadder. It's the man from her work with the cross drawing on his neck. He looks mad.

"I told you to get rid of it you stupid bitch!"

"I couldn't," she screams. "I was too far along."

He hits her, making her hair fly. She cries. He hurt her. Mommy said you only hit someone on the butt when they've done something bad. You don't hit people. It's not nice. I should tell him what Mommy said. But she said stay. "You disobeyed me! That little cunt of yours is no good to me now. You knew the rules. No pregnancies. No STDs."

"He's ours, Elliott. No one else's. Ours. I couldn't leave him. Please. I'll do anything." He pulls her to her feet and then pushes her into the wall. He's holding something black to her forehead. That doesn't look like Mommy's thermometer. She shakes her head fast, crying louder. "No. I'm sorry."

"One chance is all I give. Now you can take the barrel like you take cock," he says, and then moves the long black thing and shoves it into her mouth. A loud sound goes off when she screams, making me jump, and then red splatters around the room and on him.

"Mommy!"

He drops her on the floor and comes toward me, shoving the doors open. I move behind her clothes, but he pulls me out by the hair and tilts my head back so that he can look at me. "Jesus Christ. You look even more like me than I thought."

"What's wrong with Mommy?" I glance at her on the floor. "Is she sleeping?"

He turns me around so that I can see her. She's covered in red and something is wrong with her head. She doesn't look like Mommy anymore. He squats behind me, pulling my hair until it hurts. I cry harder. I want my mommy. "You know what it means to die, boy?"

I shake my head as he puts something sharp on the top of my neck and presses it into my skin. I scream as he pulls it down my neck, hurting me. Something wet drips. "Means you don't come back. Your mama isn't coming back, and if you don't forget you won't be either."

He lifts the knife from my skin and places it in a different place, doing the same as before. I try to kick and scream, but he holds me in place. I cry louder. I don't feel good. I trip when he pushes me. "If you ever tell I'll come find you and deal with you just like your cunt of a mother. One chance is all you get."

He stands and storms out the door, slamming it behind him. I crawl to Mommy, but quickly move away when I see her, inching under the bed and curling up. I close my eyes tight and say my prayers like Mommy does with me every night before bed. "Now I lay me down to sleep, I pray the lord my soul to keep. If I should die before I wake, I pray the lord my soul to take. Amen."

Swirls of black and light. I place my tiny hand to my neck, the wetness coating it. "I love you too, Mommy. I'm sorry I didn't protect you . . ."

Every memory assaults me as if they've been locked in a vault with a missing key. I can't breathe. People dragging me out from under the bed as I screamed for her. The club's pink neon illuminating the darkness is everywhere. The dancers—I knew them all. The bright blue sirens on the police cars against the night sky as I was put into the backseat with the lady in a suit. The sirens of the ambulance. The white sheet draped over her body as they rolled her away, and worse, my life before. A happy, chaotic, mess of a life. But it was good. We didn't have much, but she loved me. She never hurt me. And she never fucking abandoned me. She was taken, all because she kept me.

A deep growl rips from my chest. My body surges forward against a hold over and over as if I'm possessed. "Kross, calm the fuck down."

I see nothing but the memories. I only hear the gunshot. His threats. Her voice. I can hear her voice. I feel nothing but his hold as he slices a cross in my neck, tagging me. The guilt. The guilt consumes me. I just stood in that fucking closet scared. I watched him blow out the back of her head and did nothing. Nothing but forget—just like he told me to do.

An arm grips around my neck. I fight harder. Seeking freedom from my own mind. I'm stuck in purgatory. Lost in the abyss of the forgotten memories. My lungs are constricted to the point of no return. Air doesn't come. I'm going mad as it replays over and over. The blood. The brain matter.

"Stop!"

That voice. Her voice. The memories finally begin to fade. "Move!" It's her again. I can't find her in the dark. But I feel her. "Kross, baby, it's me. Delta. Remember my touch."

Light. I see light. Clear, vacant light. Lips against my lips. Body on my body. My hand traces over every contour until I can finally see her face; tear stained and worried. The air begins to come. My chest moves slowly and deeply, taking her in. The words drip from my lips like poison. "I'm just like him."

She's still crying. I just now realize she's in my arms, my hands gripping the backs of her thighs. "What?"

"I told you to get rid of it, just like he demanded for her to get rid of me."

"No, baby, you're not—"

"I'm just like him," I spit, harsher.

She looks back at Kaston, and then kisses me again, pulling me further into her world. "If that were true you wouldn't have come after me."

"She didn't abandon me."

More tears. Each one falls in a different path than the last. It's all I can concentrate on. She places her forehead against mine, until our eyes are forced to meet. "I had that feeling. It's why I went to Kaston. You're a difficult person to leave, Kross."

"She loved me."

"She loved you," she repeats.

"You love me."

"I love you."

"Our baby . . ."

"Will love you."

"But I—"

"It never has to know."

I exhale, everything calm, peaceful. She's my peace. "I remember."

"We should stay home tonight."

I remember . . .

"No." I push her off of me, my emotional armor sliding back into place. "I have plans."

"Kross . . ."

"No, Delta. Go get dressed and pack a bag. We have plans."

She looks at me, and then at Kaston. Hesitant. She doesn't want to leave. "Go!" I bark, and she turns to leave, meeting Lux at the door before they exit together.

I look at Kaston. "You good?"

"I will be. When he's a dead son of a bitch. Can you find him?"

"I will. Whatever it takes."

I gather the folders. "Good. I need some air."

I storm out of the room. Tonight and tomorrow are about her. Because after that I won't be back till I watch him take his last breath and his body is lifeless in my hands. I want blood. And I'm going after mine.

CHAPTER NINE

Kross

I stand against my truck, exhausted, wiping my hands down my face. Sleep doesn't come easy without her home. Actually, it's pretty much nonexistent. You can't miss what you don't know, but once you taste something good the craving remains. I'm living on blow and caffeine, food between. I sit up all night, waiting and watching, ensuring she's safe. Daybreak hits and I go home to shower and sleep until it's time to be back at the shop. It's never enough, because I'm so wound up and ready to see her that I'm lucky to get thirty minutes, an hour tops.

My mind is still spinning, processing all the new information. It's wearing on me mentally, but I shove it aside as the front door opens, drawing my attention. She steps out, pulling a small rolling suitcase behind her. My keys slip from my hand and hit the pavement, jaw falling. My eyes sweep from north to south, memorizing something that should never be forgotten. I've never seen her look like this: hair hanging in long, black, bouncing waves, lips the color of merlot, making her green eyes appear brighter. Her chest is bare, the deep V of the neckline coming to a point at her sternum, the tops inching close to the drop off of her shoulders. Black. The dress is black—long sleeve, fits like a glove, barely covers her ass, and legs for fucking days covered with fishnet stockings. Heels. God the heels. They match her lips.

Illegal. That outfit should be illegal.

I slide my hands in the pockets of my jacket and pull the two sides toward the center, closing it without the zipper. She finally shuts the door and walks toward me from the halted position she's in, a jacket hanging over her arm when it should be on her body. I clear my throat when she closes in on me. "You're going to freeze, Delta. We're going to be outside later."

"Lux said we have rooms. I brought warm clothes to change into later."

"You really want someone to die tonight, don't you?"

Her mouth tips as her eyes land on my crotch. "I'm assuming by that large, very noticeable bulge in your jeans that you approve?"

I grip her waist and switch our positions, pushing her against the door of my truck with my hips. "This is the shit that gets you pregnant."

"No pun intended?" She laughs, and then she becomes serious. "My body isn't going to look like this for much longer, you know. I already feel bloated as fuck."

Her previous confidence falls. "I know."

She stalls. "Are you going to still—"

"Want you?" I finish.

She's looking up at me, eyes covered in heavy makeup, wonder present in them. She nods. "It's just . . . I've . . . We never talked about this, before or since. I can try to—"

"Delta, why in the fuck are we having this conversation? There is no right answer for a man here. Why would you think of that kind of shit?"

"To prepare myself."

"Jesus." I rub my hand through the back of my hair, trying to find the words. The non-asshole version of words. Something I don't hold a skill in. "I can't . . . I don't . . ." I growl out, trying to figure out what the hell to say.

"Just tell me the truth, Kross. I can take it. You've never lied to me or spared hurting my feelings. Don't start now."

I place my palms on each side of her, demanding her full attention. "I imagine it'll be an . . . adjustment, but I don't see it making anything different. It's not like I've ever fucked a pregnant woman before. Your pussy isn't going to change, your face isn't going to change, and the bigger tits keep my cock standing on a near constant basis. You're incubating my kid. I'd like to think that makes it different than just looking at any woman sporting a large ball on her torso. I did this to you, regardless of who I've tried to blame for it."

"So you wouldn't?"

"Nope. I wasn't all that interested in sex before you, why would I be after?"

Then, as quickly as the paranoia came it leaves, and a smile is left in its place. A seductive one. I grit my teeth when she grabs my dick, not expecting it. "You wanna see red lips wrapped around this at midnight?"

My thumb rubs side-to-side over the metal of her lip ring as I look at her, trying like hell to control the only limb that has disobeyed me since the night I took her for the first time. The uncontrollable fucker has gone stupid judging by her current knocked-up state. And the newly snug confinement it's in proves it's trying hard to get inside her hot, swollen, and always-wet pussy.

Christ.

The fact that her lips are a dull finish instead of shiny is making it harder to keep my hands off of her, because her sexy little body against the side of this truck is becoming more and more appealing with every passing second. I've never seen lipstick like that before. "As tempting as that sounds, I have plans for you at midnight," I grit, trying to hold it together. "I have plans all night that don't include ripping your clothes off. Sorry, tonight the dick is off limits. We're doing . . . relationship shit."

That word feels foreign coming from my mouth, but oddly, it sounds right. She grabs my hand, inching it between her thighs until the tips are pressing underneath her underwear. Liquid heat wraps around them as she forces me into her core. Fuck me. She's so fucking swollen that my dick presses against my zipper, causing me pain. "Are you sure you want to deny me?" she asks in a voice that has my nuts tightening.

My fingers pump in and out of her against my will. She feels better with each thrust, the moans deepening with each one. "Are we taking one car or two?"

I pull my fingers out of her and straighten, attempting to push my dick down. "Thank you, Lux," she whispers in aggravation. "Cock blocker." And then fixes her clothing. I can't help but to smile down at her. "What?"

"I said tonight. My dick is off limits tonight. Technically after midnight would be tomorrow. I have every intention of fucking you into a sleep-induced coma before we call the celebrating quits."

And then she rewards me with that smile I know is completely genuine. "Thank God."

"That is if you can hang. You've been going to bed earlier lately."

When she looks at me in question I realize my slip. But then she bites the corner of her bottom lip, trying not to smile. "You've totally been stalking me, haven't you?"

"Guarding is a better word."

"I want to fuck you so hard right now."

I walk around the truck when I hear footsteps behind me. "Separate. We're riding separate," I say, while opening the truck door to the passenger side, trying to distance myself so that I can force my cock into a sleeper. I look up, Lux standing next to Delta as Kaston backs the truck out of the garage. "I have something to do first. She can text you when we get to the hotel. Delta, let's go."

She hugs Lux and whispers something in her ear, before walking toward my side of the truck as Lux walks away. "What was that?"

"Nothing," she answers, but the tone of her voice says she's lying, and not in the malicious way. No, that tone says trouble. Trouble for any man with a thirsty cock.

Delta

My heart is so full and heavy it's hard to breathe. My nervous energy has my hands twisting in my lap as we drive, sitting in silence. Not an awkward silence but a comfortable one. Happy. I'm happy. And some of the feelings thriving inside of me I don't completely understand. They're there, and I recognize them. I'm sure the rest I'll work out in time. Thoughts are racing. Decisions are being made.

I prop my elbow on the door and look out the window, trying to hide my smile with my hand. All those nights I felt like someone was watching me finally make sense. So many times I swore I was being a paranoid nut-job because I had gotten used to living with someone and was suddenly alone. I should have known it was him when I wasn't scared. Instead, I felt safe. Safer than I've ever felt since I've been on my own. "About earlier—"

His voice cutting through the warm space instantly pulls my attention. I look at him, sitting relaxed in the driver's side. I remain quiet. "I won't apologize."

He's making it really hard to remain serious, so I divert by asking a question. "How long?"

"Does it matter?"

God, I love him. "It does to me."

"Since the night I realized if I didn't I would go on a killing spree in Atlanta. Already one under my belt. Anger and anxiety are the perfect recipe for insanity. And chaos is bad for business. Sloppiness is sure to follow. Pretty much the entire time you've been gone. I didn't want you to know. I just wanted to make sure you were safe."

"How are you sleeping if you're pulling a second job as my bodyguard? Or should I say third?"

"I'm not. And I'm busy enough between you and the shop. I need to get my shit in order. Dealing will just have to wait."

Guilt consumes me. None of this was my intention by staying somewhere else. I wanted to give him the option of walking away with no strings attached. I wanted him to choose us for himself, not feel trapped because we were irresponsible with sex. "Kross . . ."

"I'm fine, Delta. Cocaine has its advantages. And I get a lot of thinking done."

"I seem to remember having a conversation once that drugs

were part of the job and nothing more."

"You are my job."

"I don't want to be your job."

He growls, as if he's aggravated. "Protecting you is. You knew what I meant."

"What you're doing . . . Many would argue that's an act of love if you're not on a payroll."

He remains silent for a few moments. He's thinking; working something out in his head. I've learned that about him. I process and understand through questions, he does it all internally. To most he just looks pissed off. I know better. If he can't work it out himself, he doesn't understand it at all. "That's something I don't understand. I don't know if I can ever . . ."

"You can," I finish, but before he can say anything more I reach over and rub my hand up and down on his crotch.

He grabs my wrist, still concentrating on the road ahead. "What are you doing? It took me a lot of bloody thoughts to make it go down." I unbuckle my seatbelt that he forced me to wear. "Delta, put that back on before we have a wreck."

He's so damn cute. The seatbelt thing just started since I've been pregnant. Already acting like a protective dad and I'm not even showing yet. I don't think he even realizes the change. It's subtle, but it's there. That fact alone melts my heart. He's not trying. It just comes naturally. Too bad for him I'm a defiant little bitch. Knees in the seat, I come across the console and nibble on his earlobe as I continue to rub, internally chanting as it quickly hardens beneath the denim. "Let me," I whisper, letting my tongue lightly run up the inside edge of his ear. "Just because I'm pregnant doesn't mean we can't have fun."

"I could wreck. Distractions like you are dangerous."

I don't miss the 'you' in that sentence. "I trust you. Even with our child." I'm already unbuttoning his jeans when he releases my wrist. His hips buck forward when I reach inside and wrap my hand around it, pulling it out, and immediately finding a slow stroking rhythm. I never craved dick until I got a taste of his.

I wrap my lips around it and plunge—a direct result of my salivating pussy. His hand fisting roughly in my hair is the push I need to consume him whole; my greedy mouth hungry for that salty serum it holds. I suck with a goal. My hand jerks with purpose.

The deep growl that tears from his chest is my cue that he's on the edge. The sharp pain of my hair being pulled at the roots tells me he's about to come. The slight pulsing of his cock prepares me to take a drink. And like the thirsty bitch that I am I hydrate, taking every single drop as he shoots his load into the back of my throat.

As I swallow and clean my lips I sit up, tucking him back into his jeans. "Take the wheel," he commands, and when I do he fastens his jeans back. "I don't want to know why you're so fucking good at that."

I can't help the smirk that occurs, because I'm about to blow his fucking mind. "Believe it or not I hated sucking dick until you. Only done it a handful of times before. I just like your dick enough to mimic enjoying my favorite frozen treat," I tease. He looks between the road and me, no enthusiasm present from my lighthearted mood; a look of unmistaken uncertainty on his face. He thinks I'm lying, or trying to inflate his ego. "Or maybe I should add that I like porn when I masturbate? Visual learning at practice just now . . . Same difference."

And with the fall of his jaw I bust out laughing. "What? Girls aren't supposed to like porn?"

"Where the fuck have you been for the last fifteen years?"

"Waiting for you?"

And then the hint of humor dissipates and he turns back to the road. "Yeah, well, I finally found you."

And with the sorrow in his words my soul cries. Because coming from anyone else that sentence would qualify as an entry in the book of most romantic lines from a guy. But from him you know it's anything but romance, because in his mind it's a very real truth. He's been stumbling around lost for a long time, but the irony in finding a lost thing is that you don't know it's lost when you find it, and that's usually the time when you need it the most.

"And you never have to let me go if you don't want to. I'm yours, Kross. We are yours."

He grabs my hand, still looking out into the distance, navigating through the heavy traffic of Atlanta. It takes him a few seconds to find a comfortable position, as if it's awkward for him to hold my hand but he's trying to hide it. "Mine."

His. Without a doubt. Everything inside of me relaxes. We're going to last. I have to believe we will. For both of us. Because I can't stand the thought of falling for another man. I want it to be him. Always and forever. Till death do us part.

CHAPTER TEN

"**S**tairs," he says, as he guides me blindfolded by his hands and stops, halting me with him. He made me close my eyes about fifteen minutes ago, and in an effort to not ruin his mood after what happened back in Kaston's office I didn't peek. It has been the longest fifteen minutes of my life, but the familiar smell reminds me of the shop.

I've always loved the smells of the shop. Kross is a big user of incense and essential oil diffusers at work. For a man he's knowledgeable and he's done his research. It's sexy as hell. And maybe that is one of the many reasons why he's so successful. He believes it relaxes the customer and gives them a better experience when dealing with pain and sometimes-long sessions, which can lead to restlessness. He changes them up, and occasionally Cassie sneaks in a more feminine aroma like Rose from his massive collection, but for the most part you'll be welcomed by scents like Vanilla and Patchouli or Sandalwood and Lavender. My favorite, though, has become Cedarwood and Jasmine, and with it being frequently used lately I think he's noticed. "Open the door in front of you."

I place my arms out, my palms colliding with a metal door. His cologne wafts through the air from him being so close to my backside. His bulky muscles and the soft cotton of his shirt feel good against me. I search for the doorknob and turn it. He pulls me back when the door touches me, allowing me to open it completely.

He then presses his body against me, inching me forward. "Climb the steps."

I do as told, extending my arms out and using my hands at my sides against the walls as a guide. I'm positive we're at work now. There's no mistaking this narrow staircase; something you don't see all that often in a business, but in tight, well-developed cities the only place left to go is up. He said he had a surprise for me, though, so I'm not sure what we're doing here. "Why are we at work when it's closed? Are you itching to get a needle in my skin?"

"You're pregnant. No."

"Such a buzzkill, you are." He sinks his teeth in the muscle running from my neck to my shoulder, sending a surge of wetness into my panties. "Fuck," I whisper as he stops me.

"Open the door." I follow instructions and step up onto the floor. "Keep them closed," he says, and then his hands fall from my eyes. I squint, trying not to let my eyelid muscles get too excited. The sudden, cool, rush of air has me wondering where he went, but in a moment's notice he returns. This time he's in front of me, grabbing my hand. I let him pull me toward the back of the room.

When we come to a stop yet again, he positions himself behind me, aligning his front to my back, snaking his hands around my waist to eliminate the space between us. I shiver when his palms take rest over my still flat belly. "Merry belated Christmas," he says. "Since I fucked it up before. Open your eyes, Delta."

Nervous, I slowly open my eyes, starting with merely softening my lids, and then finally, I raise them. "Oh my God."

Words fail me. The right words anyway. The words that would adequately describe the feelings roaming around my body as if they've lost belonging. The room is dark, except for the neon lights that show ownership of each station. Only this time, there is no vacant one. Above the station next to Kross', my name shines bright in a cursive, neon pink font. I have a place to call my own. He's going to keep me. I'm part of the family. And in his eyes I'm worthy enough to be called an artist. That means the most of all.

And suddenly, my stupid eyes start leaking—uncontrollably at that. It's like a pipe burst inside. My shoulders hunch in my attempt to stop it before I ruin my makeup. My body starts to shake. He turns me around, placing his hands on my wet face. I can only see a slight glow on his face since he left the overhead lights off, but I can tell he's concerned. "Is this a pregnancy thing?"

I start laughing, tears still streaming down my face. "Yes. No. Maybe. It's a happy thing," I finally get out. He kisses me, and with the soft touch of his lips I calm. I'm able to breathe freely, and easily, and my chest stops heaving. I wrap my arms around his waist to hold onto him. "You think I'm ready?"

"I'm not a man that does before he knows. To act on a thought isn't the behavior of a successful business owner. I know you've got the basics down. You can only tattoo so many practice skins before it becomes no different than someone learning the art of combat on a game system but doesn't know shit about actual warfare. You'll never know everything, no matter how long you shadow me, or the guys. Time and dedication separate average from the best. Mastery comes with practice, experience, and research. I know you're ready enough for me to offer student tattoos at a discounted price. It's a new thing I came up with. Protects the shop with a waiver and allows you to actually practice on a human being."

I stare at him, no longer worried about my makeup as my wet lashes continue to touch together. "For once, I don't know what to say."

"You could start with, 'Thank you, Kross. This is the best Christmas gift ever.'"

I laugh, more so at the fact that his humor is never detectable in the tone of his voice. "Thank you, Kross. This is the best Christmas gift ever."

He never reciprocates the look on my face or cracks a smile. Instead, he brushes his calloused thumb along my cheekbone, his eyes drilling into mine. He studies me, in a way that I've never been by a man. It evokes a sense of nervousness and makes me feel beautiful, wanted. "Nothing has ever had me quite like you. There's something about you I can't shake. I—"

He clamps his mouth shut before anything else can be said, and a part of me dies inside. All those months ago the only thing I wanted was to be somebody. To be the best fucking female artist there is, or at least be well on my way. I wanted a mentor. I wanted to be trained by the best. I wanted to become a legend. I wanted Kross. I still want Kross. The difference is that now more than anything else I want him to love me. I need him to need me. I long to be his . . . in every possible way there is. All he has to do is say the words. Make the decision. Ask the question. Maybe, despite everything I've ever known, there is a sliver of a romantic locked away inside, begging to be freed. "What, Kross?"

"I don't understand the way I feel."

"Explain it to me. Maybe I can help you."

He closes his eyes and shakes his head in frustration. When he opens them, his eyes are clear, distant. I've lost the moment quicker than the passing of a gust of air. "Let's go. We're going to be late."

And then he turns and once again tows me in the direction he wants me. I let him. Maybe one day he will love me. But even if he doesn't, I know I love him enough for both of us. The way he wants me is enough for me to stay. There is no greater truth than this: the broken ones hold us captive the longest. They entrap our hearts in a way we don't want them back. He captured me the moment I laid eyes on him. I'm in love with my captor. My biggest fear isn't being kept—it's being let go.

Kross

I pull her through the packed out Underground Atlanta looking for a decent spot to stand. It's body to body, the crowd hyped up and ready for some action. We're cutting it too close to midnight because of the hotel party with Kaston and Lux. Delta felt it was shitty to leave early since they paid for the tickets. In my opinion, we didn't ask for the damn tickets in the first place, so I don't see it as we owe anyone anything. This is supposed to be our night.

I was planning to get here earlier, much earlier, as in not long after we ate dinner at one of the upscale hotel restaurants—a panoramic view of the Atlanta skyline at dusk, dim lighting, and eating over candlelight with some kind of orchestra music in the background—not any music that I like. I've never felt so fucking awkward; not even at the New Year's Eve event in the ballroom, surrounded by people in cheap novelty items representing the New Year we're supposed to be bringing in.

The waiters were dressed formally, their speech way too controlled. The atmosphere was stifling and silent, reeking of money, and the food was too fancy and overpriced for someone that looks like me, but the outfit she was wearing when I picked her up didn't belong in a casual steakhouse, and the smile on her face as we stared at each other from opposite ends of the table had me keeping all thoughts to myself.

The glow across her face from the flame of the candle as it danced made it easy. She's never looked so beautiful. I remained quiet, watching her, while she mentioned repeatedly how romantic it was for me to take her to a place like that when I'm almost always void of feeling. If that's how she saw it I wasn't going to take that from her. I just thought after all the shit I've dealt her way she needed something out of the ordinary. I don't know how else to get her back home. I figured it would take something drastic.

I continue pushing through the never-ending maze created by so many bodies. People are screaming, taking selfies, and binging on boos and God knows what else. Body count in this magnitude puts me on the edge. Words like Facebook, Twitter, and Instagram are being thrown around like confetti. I'm sure most of these people will post the same damn videos on YouTube later. Females are actually dressed more season appropriate out here compared to the scraps of fabric labeled as dresses I saw inside the hotel. Flasks and cups are out in every size and color. My eyes set on the place I want to be.

I stop suddenly when a drunk girl in heels stumbles in front of me, spilling her drink all over the pavement. She looks up, a huge clown-like smile plastered on her face. "Fuck, the guys are hot here. I'm Candi, and I'm interested."

"I'm not. Keep moving."

"Your loss, sexy. You'll be missing out on probably the easiest lay you've ever had. Tourist goals."

Delta smashes into my backside, and shortly after her voice sounds. "Back up, asshole."

I turn around, agitated, my eyes setting on the 'asshole' that has his dick practically glued to her ass and his lips pressed to her ear. I can smell the beer from here. She rips her hand from mine and grips his face in her hand, shoving him backward. "In your dreams, loser. Fuck off before you regret it. You reek."

Against my better judgment I keep my mouth shut. My temper needs to remain under control in a public place where cops are at every corner, watching and waiting for someone to fuck up. If I'm going to leave her for a few days I need to know she can take care of herself, because I can't take her with me. Not for this. This is something that is long overdue, and as much as I'd like to pretend it's been in the back of my mind, it's been anything but. I finally have some answers. I finally remember things. I no longer feel foreign in my own mind.

I've thought about that fucking file about every ten seconds since we left Kaston's house—through dinner, through the hotel party, and on the way here. This is something I have to deal with. I have no chance at giving her a normal relationship if I don't handle this. Twenty-six years are riding on it. Kaston is the only one that could tell my mind was elsewhere. An emotional cripple has some advantages in times like this. She needs to have fun, because I've been an angry dick to her long enough.

"Come on, girl. I know you're easy. Look at you. I bet you spread them legs for a lot of guys."

My head snaps to the short, playboy wannabe fucker and before I can stop myself his neck is in my grasp, my hand closing like a pair of pliers. The pressure buildup from his lack of air gives me a rush. His nails clawing at my hand sends me into overdrive. Everything blurs except for one thing: him. I want him dead. I want to be the reason his soul is disconnected from his body.

"Kross, it's not worth it. Baby, let him go." Her voice cuts through the silence in my head, enunciating the word 'baby'. And suddenly nothing is silent any more. The celebratory screams and laughter return. The thousands of conversations mix together in the air. When I glance over, the sea of people are still present, most not paying any attention. His face is pale and his lips are turning blue. My size dominates his by a lot.

I pull him forward. "Touch my girl or talk to her like that again and I'll leave your body parts scattered all over this goddamn city."

My hand instantly releases its hold. I watch with regret as he rushes away. I can count on one hand the times I've let someone live in that state. When I make up my mind there is no going back. That dumb fuck got lucky tonight. Should have killed him. I flinch at the feel of skin against my skin, a palm on my stomach. Then I relax when the familiar touch registers. *Memorize my touch.*

I look at her. She wraps her arms around me and her smile is long gone. Her eyes are dull and the outer edges are sloped downward. "Are you okay? Maybe this was a bad idea. Do you want to go back to the hotel party?"

She shakes her head and tightens her hold around me. *One, two, three . . . Delta. Delta's touch is different. It's . . . wanted.* I instantly relax, my hands going for her face, tilting her head back so that I can see her more clearly in the limited light. "He's just a dickweed, Kross. Likely a slim jim—two to four inch skinny dick that's not visibly appealing or fulfilling. I'm used to guys like him. What I'm not used to is the way you just looked. I know we've talked about things, but I've never witnessed that. What would have happened had I not been here?"

One thought processes. "A fucking slim jim? Jesus, who comes up with this shit? Ruin my liking of a perfectly good protein snack. Maybe it's because of my lack of friends, but I've never known guys to have the same views of pussy as apparently girls have of dick. It's a wonder any of you get laid at all with those kinds of cut-downs."

"Are you seriously taking his side after you were a second away from choking him to death?"

"No. He was a prick. I would have gladly castrated him for what he said and pressed against you. I'm stating the obvious. To most guys, their dicks are sacred. Those are suicide-worthy attacks. Not all men have swords in their pants."

She smiles. Finally. A brief laugh follows. I like it better when she smiles. She then presses closer, before grabbing my dick through my jeans. "Like you?

"I wouldn't know. I don't sit around comparing my cock."

"Oh, but I know you do. And that's all that matters."

"You didn't know that before I fucked you. Most would call that luck of the draw." Her smile changes. "What?"

"There is a lot about women you don't know. We always notice. I had you sized up by the second week. The memory is very clear. I was wearing those black denim cut-offs and the mutilated sleeveless band tee shirt with the bandeau underneath to cover my boobs. I was prepping your station for your first appointment; nervous as fuck when the door opened. It was the first time we were alone in the studio after I started. When you walked in that morning you took one look at me and stopped at the door, before stomping over to your station like I had pissed you off. It seemed like I did that often. You were hard, moody as fuck. God, that fucking bulge. I was so wet I had to go to the bathroom. You thought I didn't notice, but I did. Even saw you trying to casually press it down when I wasn't looking. I likely would have let you fuck me then had you made an attempt. I didn't think you were ever going to try to get in my pants. And when you finally did . . ."

"It had been building for way too long," I admit, horny as fuck in the middle of all these people as I replay the memory, and can't do shit about it. Suddenly, I'm regretting my plans.

"And it was worth every degrading thing you said," she whispers.

"Degrading?"

She laughs. "You aren't the most complimentary person. Or the most filtered. You have very set ideals, especially in regards to stripping. Rather, you outright made me feel like a whore, but it was glorious."

"Maybe I was too harsh. I understand now why I had such a problem with it. It was because of her. My . . . Rachel. I was acting out subconsciously. I was an angry person all the fucking time. You didn't belong in there."

"Too harsh? Is that your version of an apology?" The laughter in her tone and the grin on her face proves she doesn't expect one.

"Are you sure you don't want to leave? You're quivering. I told you I'd be shit at dates."

She pulls in closer, laying her cheek against my torso. "No. I want to stay here. This is us. Our style. It's not often you want to do something like this. I'm wearing jeans and a jacket. Even a beanie. I'll be fine."

I wrap my arms around her, trying to warm her shaking body. It's a cold one tonight. Every breath visible in the black of night. I look around as I hold her close. People watching—it's something I've always done since I'm not much for social interaction or talking. Friends, couples, large and small groups. There is one common denominator: they all look happy. Something I've never been.

I lay my chin on the top of her head, freely thinking. It's not the first time I've realized that with her I'm the most peaceful. I'm happy, if that's what this is. Less angry for sure. But there is a void. That void is one that she can fill, because she already has. We're at a crossroads. It's the close of one year and the beginning of another. With the knowledge of my past, maybe it's time I change my future. Because once someone loved me, even if only for a little while, and that truth is enough to let go of some of the pain and some of the anger. I take a deep breath, letting the cold air invade my lungs, and then I pull her closer on exhale. "I miss you, Delta."

She pulls away and looks up at me, clearly confused. "What do you mean?"

It's time I stop being a pussy, before someone else is calling her his girl. "I miss you. All of you. I miss you at home. I miss you in my bed. Our bed. Come back home."

"Kross . . ."

The crowd starts the countdown as the giant peach begins to fall. "Ten, nine, eight, seven, six . . ."

"I love you, Delta."

Her mouth falls, and following right behind are the tears as they make a trail down her face. "Are you sure?" she whispers.

I pick her up, forcing her legs to wrap around my waist. "Yeah, I'm sure. I think I've been in denial for a while, but fuck all if this isn't it, so put me out of my misery. Come home. I can't promise I won't fuck up. If someone touches you I'll still want to beat him to a pulp. I'll probably swear a lot, even when I'm not supposed to. When it comes to understanding something obvious in regards to feelings I'll likely always flunk, so if I say something in regards to the baby or this pregnancy that makes you want to run, just punch me in the dick instead. It'll hurt a lot less."

". . . four, three, two, one. Happy New Year!"

Her warm lips press against mine in a rush. Her tongue seeks a connection but only briefly. Then she pulls away. "Is that a yes?"

She laughs. "Oh it's a hell yes. Have you not figured it out yet? That's all I was waiting on. To know you loved me and weren't just serving some kind of honorable manly duty."

"Thank fuck. Though a hint would have been nice."

I kiss her this time, and the popping in the sky as the fireworks go off break us apart. She looks up, but I look at her. I've never been as curious about a woman as I am with her. She's holding onto the back of my neck, leaning back as she looks up at the onyx sky. The sounds remind me of gunfire. But the glittery sparks mirrored in her eyes are something more. Magical, if there was such a thing.

"Isn't it beautiful?"

"You are."

She looks down at me, a smile on her face. "Happy New Year, Kross."

"Happy New Year, Delta."

She leans in. "I think this is going to be the best one yet."

"You think so? Why's that?"

"Because we have a family."

"Yeah . . ."

"Kross."

"What?"

"Take me back to the room. There's something I want you to do."

"And that something is?"

"Make love to me."

Fucking love. Well I'll be damned . . .

CHAPTER ELEVEN

Delta

His lips touch down on my body, marking a place every inch from neck to pelvis. "That feels nice," I state in my half-asleep state of mind. But then his tongue dips between my legs, quickly drawing me out of my slumber. I try to sit up, but he holds my legs open, continuing his amazing and completely unfair assault. I was not prepared. Had I known he would be giving me an orgasmic wakeup call I would have at least done a hygiene check first; something I've never cared about with men prior to Kross. But he is a man of few words, and one that possesses a lot of skill, especially where women are concerned.

I grip his hair, trying to push him away but pull him toward me at the same time. I'm a war within myself, but he's a lot stronger than me, and he doesn't let up until I'm coming hard against his tongue. I finally give up the fight, riding out the strong high resulting from the burst of orgasm that crept up on me, and before it's completely gone he roughly turns me over, positioning me on all fours.

I just now notice that he's completely naked and ready to go, already aligning himself against me, and with one hard thrust he buries himself inside, shoving me forward until my hand grabs at the headboard to prevent my head from plowing against it. "Fuck, yes."

The sting on my skin as he slaps my ass proves he's not in a playing mood. He's agitated, but I'm not sure why. With every hit of his rock hard pelvis against my backside I can feel what will later be bruising. He's fucking like a man on a mission, and instead of wading in the shallows he's swimming in the deep. Every time he grazes my cervix it takes my breath away as the searing pain shoots through my abdomen. I clench down on the headboard and grab my breast in the opposite hand, pinching my nipple to offset some of the feelings parading through my body.

His hands lock down at the junction of my legs and torso as he quickly finds my G-spot, and with the gyrating rhythm against it I effortlessly come, my pussy pulsating around him as the moaning screams begin. I chance a glance, trying to hold my eyes open with the overwhelming pleasure racking my body. Every tattoo is mobile as his body rocks against me, the muscles in his abdomen contracting with every thrust.

Finally he holds me against him, hard and heavy as a growl tears from his chest, and with concentration I can feel him release himself inside of me. My body is covered in a mixture of our sweat to match, and without pulling out he leans forward, kissing my shoulder blade. I shiver when a sudden burst of air blows down on my wet body from the heater being off.

He runs his hand slowly up my front, momentarily stopping on the beginning of a bump, before continuing on until his hand is firmly clenched around my breast. "Do you know how good your pussy feels since you've been knocked up? It's like a personal heater for my cock."

His dirty talk sends chills down my spine. His voice alone is enough to instill fear in the bravest person. I turn my head, allowing my ear to brush against his lips. "Mm."

I squeeze around him, tightly enveloping his dick before it completely softens inside of me. "Careful, beautiful. I have a lot left in me." He pulls out of me and turns me around until I'm standing on my knees. Even soft he's impressive below the belt. And it's all mine. His eyes divert to my stomach. It doesn't help that we've been sleeping mostly naked almost nightly since I moved back in—a direct result of sharing a bed again for the last month. We're a couple of horny rabbits. I love it. I've never gotten so much raw heat out of him. "I haven't noticed that, until today. It's barely there, but it's hard."

My hands reflexively try to cover it, insecure, but he stops me. "It started off as bloating. I've felt it for a while, internally, but I won't be able to hide it from you any longer. It feels like an inflated balloon in my gut. With the right clothing I still have a while before anyone else notices."

"Why would you be trying to hide it from me?"

"Because I know you're not thrilled about it. Out of sight out of mind kind of thing, I guess. I feel like it's going to be a constant reminder slapping you in the face."

"What would be the point in trying to forget about it? We made it. It's done. There is nothing we can do about it. I chose to accept it when I chose to go after you. As long as it doesn't change you I'll come around."

"But—"

He grabs my thighs and transitions me to my back, my hair splaying across the pillow from being caught off guard. "No buts. When I woke up I felt it. It was there, under my hand. I've been thinking about it for the last hour before the thoughts of my kid in there made me too horny to let you sleep. You're now untouchable. And that vamps up my testosterone levels way too much. Fucking ironic isn't it? Something I hated so much in the beginning now turns me on. We're having a kid. You rarely mention it or draw attention to it. It's always me, usually in hindsight. Stop walking around on eggshells around me about it. We might as well mention it, look at it, and somehow prepare for it like we would prepare for a fucking hurricane. When it hits everything will be different, and that's fine, as long as you and me stay the same."

"I just don't want to lose you from too much change too soon, now that things are the way they are," I say, ashamed I even feel this way when I was strong enough to walk away after an ultimatum.

He surprises me by kissing the highest point of my belly. He doesn't immediately pull away either. I stare at a pile of brown hair, already at seven seconds in my head when he moves to become eye level with me. Then he looks at me with a fierce expression, before saying something so profound it confiscates my air. "The night I killed for you was my promise to stay. No oath can be broken when sealed with blood."

My body surges forward and my lips steal his. I wrap around him, coercing him between my legs. I'll never tire of the way his thick body feels against my petite one. "Want to do it again?"

He bites at my lip, before pulling away. "I have something to tell you."

The seriousness that washes over him concerns me. "What is it?"

"I have to leave for a while."

My brows crease. "Where are you going? And how long is a while?"

"I have to go back to Illinois. Business. I'm not sure how long I'll be. As long as it takes."

"Well why didn't you say so? Can I go? I kind of miss the guys."

"Not that kind of business."

Dread pools in the pit of my stomach. He's being vague. One thing I've fallen in love with in regards to Kross is his honestly and the fact that he holds nothing back. I don't like this secretive side. "Then what kind of business would have you shutting me out when you've taken me to fucking deals before? Before I was even okay with it."

"This is bigger than you. You're fucking pregnant. I don't want you stressing over it."

I look at him, anger building from the seed of fear planted. I roll out from under him before he can trap me, quickly making my way to the connecting bathroom. I hear it when his feet hit the floor and then he comes following closely behind. He pushes the door open with force as I enter, the knob slamming against the wall. "Delta," he barks.

"I need to get ready for work," I say, turning on the shower. As steam billows, I step inside, hoping he will leave me alone. When I'm angry and have no control over what I'm angry about, it's best to just sulk it off. No such luck. He steps inside behind me, pulling the glass door closed. "What do you want? You said your piece."

"Don't be a bitch."

I spin around. Water is running down his front like a waterfall gliding over rocks, making every tattoo glossy instead of matte. Oh, for all that is holy, why must his body look like that? "Seriously? Do you have special privileges that I'm not entitled to? You're an asshole on the regular. This is one of those times when I want to punch you in the dick like you gave me permission to do. We're a couple. You've trusted me with everything else. Why not now? You brought me into this life. And because I wanted you I overlooked things. Because I love you I'm a part of it. You don't just fucking tell me you're leaving with no date of return and then keep me in the dark. We're supposed to be in this together."

He steps forward, cornering me in the tile shower, his palms planting on the wall to each side of me. "You want to know where I'm going? Fine. I was trying to protect you mentally. You seem to be skittish where breaking the law is concerned, and your conscience is a hell of a lot more active than mine. That file that Kaston had on me—I asked him to track down the bastard I share DNA with. The one that coincidentally I'm a lot fucking like. I'm going to kill him, just like he killed my mother. He sentenced me to a life in Hell, so I'm going to send him there with the cunt that raised me, raped me, and ruined me. It's taken Kaston a while to get a lead, but I finally got his latest location this morning. It's why I was awake. I have to go."

Panic starts to rise. "Take me with you."

He shakes his head. "No."

"Why not? You have for everything else."

"Do you think I'm going to hand him my weakness on a fucking platter? You make it more dangerous. I need you here where I know you're safe."

"Can't you just let it go? Please. Stay here with me."

"I can't. I'll be back when I'm done disposing of his body."

My fear of something happening to him has my entire body in a state of distress, grasping at straws. "You want me to talk about this baby? I will. What if something happens? What if you end up in prison? Or worse? We both grew up without a father, Kross. Don't do that to our baby. Please. Stay. It's not worth the risk."

He leans forward, his large body towering over me, his hand gripping my chin firmly so that I won't turn away. "I need to do this, Delta," he says softly. "For us. Including the baby."

His eyes are sincere, his expression raw. There is nothing hard present in them right now. He's unguarded, which is rare for him. My confusion doubles. "Why?"

"I need to free myself from the one thing that cripples me. There is no future without closure from the past. He's the one link to the memories, the torment, and the reason I'm so fucked up. I'm tired of the mind games. If you want me to be the best man for you, to come to terms with this baby, then this is something I have to do. I realized how much I was like him when the memory came back, knowing I, too, ordered you to abort our kid. I can't be like him anymore. He has to die, Delta, or I'll never live in peace."

My heart is overcome with heartache. I'm torn between the man I love and our child. I can't send him off, but I can't ask him to stay. So I'll be his support, regardless of how I feel. I wrap my arms around him and stand on my tiptoes to increase my height. He uses it as a cue to pick me up, holding me against the shower wall. "Some of your behavior may be similar to his, but I think you're more like your mother. You care. From the beginning, you've cared. And that's what scares me the most, because the opposite is what makes him lethal. Do what you must and then come back to me, but please don't ask me to stay behind again."

And then he kisses me in a way he never has before: with finality.

I watch him as he pulls out a large black duffel bag from the closet next to the basement entry. I follow him down the stairs into the basement, nails shredding between my teeth as I watch him quickly pack it with weapons of every size and make. He's not preparing to silently take out one man, he's preparing for an ambush. My nerves are on edge with every second that passes. I've already forgotten about how it felt when he made love to me in the shower. "How are you even going to take all of that if you're flying?"

He doesn't stop. "It'll meet me there. Moving arsenal is what I do best."

My eyes are stinging from the tears building up that I'm trying to hold back. It all is becoming so much more real now. He walks to a bookshelf and moves a book, revealing a keypad. Ten digits and he's pulling the entire shelf open like a door. A huge safe comes into view with its own lock. He opens it. My eyes widen when he pulls out stacks of cash, then closes it back, locking it and positioning everything back into place as if it doesn't exist.

He closes the duffle bag and walks toward me, handing me one stack of money and a bank bag. I stare at it. "Take it."

"No. What's this for?"

He shoves the bank bag at me first. "Credit cards in your name I authorized a while back and had put up. Codes to the safe if something were to happen. Everything you need is in there if I don't come back, including GPS coordinates to cash stash houses and information for offshore bank accounts. Spare keys to everything." He then hands me the thick, bank-wrapped stack of hundreds. "Cash. For an emergency."

I shake my head, refusing to take it, but he forces it into my hands. "No. What the fuck, Kross? This was supposed to be something easy. You go, do, you come back. Simple. Whatever this fucked up shit is was not part of it. You're scaring me." The tears disobey my command to stay and spill from my eyes in thick cascading waves. "I didn't agree to this."

He grips behind my neck and pulls me toward him. "Look at me."

I shake my head; my eyes clenched shut as the cries of fear consume me. "Delta, look at me." I finally do as he says, my eyes sore from the fast, uncontrollable crying. "I watched him murder my mother without hesitation at a young age. Why he had a conscience when it came to me I'm unsure. He's the kingpin of a massive underground prostitution ring he hides with strip clubs. He's smart or he'd be in prison. I told you, we're a lot alike in ways. He didn't get that way by playing it safe. I'm not stupid or overly confident. He's either going to die or I am."

"Why are you doing this to me? To us?"

My shoulders slump and I sob, holding everything to my chest. Just when I thought everything was perfect we end up here. I should have known better.

Stupid, stupid girl.

"Delta, I need you to listen to me."

It's hard to pull air into my lungs. "Please don't go."

"Be my eyes and ears, baby. You can sit with Remington until I get back when you go to the shop. You can start tattooing on your own when I return. Never go anywhere alone unless you're here at home. I have cameras all over this fucking property. Johnny's number is in your phone. One single thing seems off you call him. Got it?" I nod, my entire body numb. "You can track my location on the app just like I can yours. I already programmed everything before I gave you the phone. I'll leave it on until I'm forced to turn it off for your protection. If something happens . . ." I cry harder. He squeezes the back of my neck. "If something happens to me everything is yours. Kaston will help you figure out the details. Take care of our baby."

I wrap my arms around him and cling on with every ounce of strength I have, my body quivering. This is a nightmare, every woman's worst-case scenario. He forces me to look at him. "I love you, girl. One thing I thought I'd never do, and that's all you. Now I know there is always something worth living for, no matter how bad things are." He kisses me and pulls away too soon. "I gotta go before I lose track of him."

I hold on tighter, but he forcefully separates us and makes his way toward the stairs. My heart is pounding against my chest. "Kross, wait. There is something I need to tell you," I force out when he's already halfway to the top. He looks like a fucking God up there, perched on top of the world. That's Kross. He dominates everything with only his existence. "I love you. I-I knew who you were when I scheduled my tattoo appointment. I sought you out from the first time I read about you in that article of that tattoo magazine. I knew I had to know you, to meet you in the least. You're not the crazy one. It's me. I'll always love you, all of you—the beautiful, the bad, and the broken. Now I need you. I lied. I can't do this alone. I need you to come back. Promise me you'll be back."

He smiles down at me—that sexy smirk as if he's already one step ahead. "I knew everything there was to know about you the night you and Lux walked into my studio. It was easy once I had your information sheet. I knew then I wasn't letting you completely walk away. Lux just gave me an opening and I took it."

More tears fall. "I'm madly in love with you."

"Tell me again when I get back."

Then he continues up the stairs and disappears through the door, leaving me completely alone. I stare at it, in shock, my face soaked in a salty concentrated liquid. My brain finally restarts and I take off running, but as I open the front door his truck is already turning out of the driveway onto the road.

I slam it back, angry and hurt. I don't feel like doing a fucking thing. I'm exhausted, and I'm all alone in this big house. I feel like I could sleep for a week. Kross always had a way of making me forget about the pregnancy symptoms, and with his departure they're all coming back full force. I want to sit and chain-smoke a pack of cigarettes. The craving is intense. One surely wouldn't hurt. What am I thinking? Kross would kill me. A bath. That's what I need, and it's safe for all attending parties.

CHAPTER TWELVE

Kross

I stand against the brick wall at the back of the shop, my boot perpendicular to the mortar lines, already waiting with my hands in the front pocket of my hoodie when the metal door flies open. His booted heavy footsteps descend until he's matching my position, lighting a cigarette. "That shit's going to give you cancer."

Deep laughter fills the cold, night air, preceding the thick, cloud-like smoke. Nausea settles in the pit of my stomach with the recognition of the familiar smell, the memories of that cunt flooding back to the present as if she never left. Like I always do when they consume me, I ignore them, hoping for a better one of similar circumstances to quickly replace it, like Delta sneaking a smoke when she thought I wasn't around. The only reason I pretended not to know about it was because I found peace in watching her during those times. She always looked like she was lost in a world of her own. Her full lips wrapped around that filter were almost sexy enough to overcome my repulsion with smoking. "Like you would care. Then I wouldn't be around to give you shit about your old lady. Wesson is the one you should really be pissed at. He actually did have a thing for her in the beginning. I think he's just too scared of you to admit it."

"As he should be. And I would care when I'd be wasting time looking for your replacement."

"I can imagine the agitation. I'm a hard guy to replace."

I turn to look at him, a gush of air pushing into the hood of my hoodie and running down my back. "Cut the shit, Remington, or we'll be finding out a lot sooner."

"Always threatening my livelihood." He takes one final drag and stomps it out, blowing that toxic waste into the clean air. "Happy now? What'd you want to see me about, boss man? Didn't think I'd be seeing you today since Cassie had to reschedule your entire appointment list for this week. She's been bitchy all day. I was about to close up."

"You got priors. Robbery and Grand Theft Auto." He tenses, glancing around, eyes suddenly wide as he scopes out the parking lot. "No one's here. Just you and me."

"I did my time back in Boston. I left that shit behind. I need this job, Kross." He takes a deep, stress-filled breath. "I know you don't like me much. Manager promotion was a shock. The shit with Delta—it was just me fucking around. I got a kid. It's a long-ass story, but I can't fuck up. They just let me start seeing her."

"Never said I was firing you."

He relaxes. "How long have you known?"

"Since I hired you. I know everything about my artists."

"Then why bring it up now?"

"Because it's just now useful information to me."

"How is that information useful?"

"There are reasons why I prefer to hire dirty artists over clean. A large percentage of my staff has a record. At some point that may be of value to me; like now. And I know those that don't always obey the law understand what it means to be a rat. That it will get you fucking killed. I have to leave for a while. There is a shipment coming in tomorrow at midnight. I need you to be at my warehouse to receive it. If you do there will be a cut in it for you."

"What kind of shipment?"

"The kind I'll gut you over should details leak. That's all you need to know."

"Is this the kind I could do hard time for?"

"Only if you get caught."

"What if I don't want the risk?"

"Then you can keep on pissing away your commission on broads and booze while your daughter calls someone else Daddy. Which doesn't matter to me. Though I hear college is expensive these days. Ten grand for a few hours of your precious whoring time could cut out a fraction of that."

He anxiously pulls at his hair, pushing off the wall, before lighting another cigarette. "Fuck! Give me the details."

I pull a folded sheet of paper from the pocket of my hoodie and hand it to him. He opens it, before the confusion mars his face. "It's blank."

I straighten, preparing to leave. "I don't operate in a way that could easily fuck me over should you have butter fingers. Find a black light and the instructions are there. I need one more thing."

"What?"

"I need you to look after Delta while I'm gone. She trusts you, for whatever damn reason, and if I send Kaston she'll know I asked. I need her happy. I need her stress free." I hand him several hundreds, but clamp down when he goes to take it, not letting go just yet. "And completely unaware of this transaction. Take her out if you must. What I don't need is her moping around because I'm gone. Do shit friends do, but if you so much as graze an inappropriate part of her I'll slit your throat just enough to keep you alive and throw you into the gulf for the sharks."

I release the money. "Fine, but why does Delta need a babysitter? Have you not seen her? For such a little person she's a badass. I think she could take care of herself."

"She's carrying my fucking kid. That's why," I say, catching him off guard. A look of understanding slides into place and he shoves the money into the pocket of his jeans. "Follow directions to the letter and there will be more."

I begin to walk off, leaving him behind. I stop to look over my shoulder, remembering one last thing. "Oh, and Remington . . ."

"Yeah, boss?"

"Your agreement is your signature on a contract. My business stays my business. If you so much as breathe a word I'll cut out your tongue and send it to your little girl on her birthday. Bring someone and you sign their death certificate. If you think I'm bluffing I can introduce you to others before you that learned the hard way."

I continue to my truck, not bothering to see if he's still standing there. I have a plane to catch. Since I left Delta this morning I've been with Kaston all day on recon, tying up loose ends. Everything is on schedule. The only thing left is to find that motherfucker and hand him over to Lucifer himself. Kaston offered to do the job for me—baby gift or some shit—but I turned it down. I don't need someone to do my dirty work. My hands have been bloodstained for a long time. I want to look in his eyes when he takes his last breath. And when the world as he knows it ceases to exist, as did mine all those years ago, I want to be the one that changed it all . . . just like him.

Then, when it's all over, I can get back to my girl and try like hell to give her a semi-normal life. God knows that's not as easy as it sounds for a guy like me. But that kid has no chance if I don't do this. I won't risk that kind of history repeating itself. It has shitty DNA coming from both sides. One side has to dominate the other, and I'll die fighting before I let that fuck's reign . . . again.

CHAPTER THIRTEEN

Della

The brutal memories come at me as I drive down the main street of my hometown. I almost pass by Ella's place, before deciding to stop, turning into The Watering Hole and parking my Infinity in the front row. Ella knows everything that goes on in this 'too small' small town. Unlike Lux who was babysitting her mom on the regular for years, I haven't been back once since I left, and that is going to warrant some information that I can't get on my own, because God knows she's not likely home.

I grab my purse from the passenger seat, staring at the dated building that's cherished by so many people in this town. Responsible for the only live music for miles around and the weekend entertainment for many, it's impacted a lot of lives over the years. Compared to the bars and clubs in Atlanta it's just some redneck honky-tonk, but to the people that can't get away it beats sitting at home on a Friday night watching reruns and eating one of the few fast food places in town. I'm not sure what's going to happen when Ella can no longer run it, since she cared about it too much to actually build a life of her own; no kids to leave it to.

I glance around, taking in my surroundings for the first time in years. I haven't driven these streets in so long, but like lyrics of an old song, you pick it back up as if you visited them recently. Ella's place marks the fork for what side of town you want to be on. I place my hand over the small bump covered easily by my clothing. "This is the place I grew up, Peanut. I know it's not much. When we're gone you won't even miss it. I know I haven't. On the way, just over the county line, we covered a majority of what's here from the three-generation family-owned hardware store to a pharmacy and small medical clinic sitting opposite sides of the road from each other, and then there were the gas stations on every corner and the two dollar stores you can find in almost every tiny town, all located on the same main drag."

I let the photographic memory of the town map out in my mind. "The only thing we didn't see in the matter of a five minute drive was the post office and school down that stretch of roadway over there. I'm not sure I'm ready to venture down there yet. My mother works there. She's the postmaster. It totally makes sense for her to have such a title. Damn workaholic. Oh, I forgot about the little burger joint right off the highway. It has the best chili around. It's a wonder I was able to hold any kind of figure growing up with all of that sloppy goodness. There are a few more dine-in and drive-thru restaurants and small businesses speckled throughout, but you get the picture. Nothing fancy in these parts."

I take a deep breath, preparing myself to go in, when Kross' ringtone starts sounding on my phone, making me jump. "Shit."

I dig through my purse, looking for it. It's been three damn days since he left, and all I've gotten is a text here and there. If it wouldn't absolutely kill me I'd ignore his call to give him back a little of what I've gone through.

I finally pull it out, the photo I took of him sleeping in his boxer briefs with his tattoo-covered forearm draped across his eyes on the front. The sight makes me miss him even more. "Peanut, don't tell your daddy I'm taking you in a bar. He's the judgmental type. We both know I don't need that kind of anger in my life."

I slide the green button, pulling the phone to my ear. "Hello."

"Where the fuck are you?"

Fuck! I mouth, trying to decide if I should lie or tell the truth. This is Kross we're talking about. Tell the truth, because chances are he already knows. But that doesn't mean I'm not going to make him wait before I freely give him the info. "So it's been THREE damn days since you left, with no call to say 'hey baby, how is your day' or 'I miss you and I'm fine', yet you can randomly pull up your little tracking app to see that I'm not in Atlanta and just call me up to make demands? It ain't happening, sexy; not in this lifetime."

"It's for your own good. Where are you, Delta?"

"I think we both know that's a rhetorical question, because your little GPS friend has already pinpointed exactly where I am."

"Delta . . ."

"Kross."

"I know what fucking town you're in. Even got the name of the street perfectly spelled out for me. My question is why the hell are you there and why did you choose to wait till I'm gone to go there?"

My head falls against the steering wheel, before softly hammering against it in frustration. "Ok, fine, I'll tell you, but promise not to judge me, k?"

"I can't make that kind of promise without knowing all the facts."

He's going to kill me . . .

"I came to see my mom."

Silence comes through the phone. It's so quiet you could hear a pin drop. As a matter of fact, a sound begins coming across the line. It sounds like a . . . "What is that noise?"

The blade stops slinging open from its housing. I listen carefully. A scraping noise occurs, but it's distinct, as if he's rubbing the blade of his knife against the stubble on his cheek. "Kross . . ."

"Why are you going to see that bitch? And without me there at that?"

"I just started thinking while you were gone. We're going to be parents soon. Well, sooner than we planned. And with every passing day that I remember our baby is growing inside of me and how that makes me feel, the more confused I become that she wouldn't want me. Do you know that she hasn't tried to contact me once since I moved away? What kind of mother forgets about the child she lived with for eighteen years? I need closure, Kross, like you."

"And what if she tries to hurt you?"

"She won't hurt me physically. At least not more than I can take. A slap to the face was about as bad as it got. She was a shitty mom, but she wasn't like that. She's only ever had the power to hurt me emotionally and mentally, and now, so much time has passed she really doesn't even have that. I want some answers so I can move on and we can live our life with no questions."

I hear him growl into the phone. "Look in the glove compartment."

I lean over the console and flip open the compartment. There is a stack of various items related to the sale of my car, including my insurance, but what wasn't previously there is a silver and Tiffany

Blue pistol lying on top."

"What is it?"

"I hope that's a fucking joke."

I roll my eyes. "I meant what kind? Why the hell is it in here? Those type questions."

"Because I don't trust other people. That's why it's in there. It's a Ruger LC9s."

"So you put an illegal gun in my car?"

"No, that one's registered. Not all of my guns are illegal, Delta, just the ones I sell . . . or use for illegal activity."

"Well, okay then. You could have just said it was there. I didn't have to look at it. The likelihood of me using it is slim."

"No. If you're going to be there without someone then put it in your purse."

"Kross, I grew up here. I don't need a gun."

"Put the fucking gun in your purse or I'm sending Kaston to pick you up."

I move it from the glove compartment to my purse, verbally voicing my frustration the entire way. "It's in there. Happy now?"

"Somewhere between happy and rage."

"What are you doing?"

"Stakeout."

"I'm not going to ask many questions, because I don't want to know, but when are you coming home?"

"When his soul is on fire."

"Why is it taking so long?"

"Crime takes time."

"I miss you."

"I'll be home soon."

I glance up to Ella standing in the doorway of the bar, staring at me. "Kross, I gotta go. I'll let you know when I'm headed back home. Love you. Be safe."

I disconnect the call and toss my phone in my purse, before quickly getting out of my car and locking it up. Her face is void, staring between the car and me. Hell, maybe she doesn't recognize me. Sure, it has been a while and I have a lot more tattoos now, but I pretty much look the same.

I take two steps forward and then her hard demeanor cracks, a smile breaking out. "Well I'll be damned. I thought you had forgotten us around these parts."

"Not the ones worth remembering."

She glances at my car again. "I almost got my shotgun out. Thought you were some of those rich city folk trying to persuade me to sell my bar. They've been at it for about a month now. Investors wanting to tear down this place and build a strip of office buildings to lease out. They'll have to wait till I'm dead and gone. Some things are worth more than money."

I smile at her, remembering all the times she took Lux and I into her arms and treated us like a real mother would, because the ones we shared DNA with were out partying, a lot of times in this very bar, acting like a couple of teenagers with no offspring. "It's good to know some things haven't changed. How you been, Ella?"

"Not as good as you apparently. What happened to the old Volkswagen?"

"Boyfriend scrapped it."

"That's a sin. It was an antique."

She holds open her arms, waiting for me to fall in. I do, and with one breath I'm taken back. Familiarity swarms around us— her mint shampoo, the light smell of Marlboro on her skin, only noticeable in close proximity, and the fresh clean smell of fabric softener from her clothes. I squeeze her tight. "Even the best things must come to an end."

She pulls away, her playful expression back. "Why do I have a feeling we're no longer talking about the car?"

"You always had a knack for reading between the lines."

"And I'm guessing you didn't stop by to see your mother before coming by?"

"Your guess would be a good one."

She takes a deep breath and then wraps her arm around my shoulders. "Come inside and have a seat. I'll have the boys in the kitchen make you a burger and fries on me. I'll even throw in an order of fried pickles with ranch. It always was your favorite.

My mouth starts watering at the mention of pickles. "I should have come back a long time ago."

"You're going to need something to keep your mouth busy for a while. There are things to say. I've kept my mouth shut long enough, but a lot of things have changed since you left and I think it's time that you know."

She pulls me inside. As I cross over the threshold something in the air changes. And that something fills me with dread.

I stand on the walkway, staring at the wooden front door of the house in my old neighborhood. It's hard to believe I'm back at the place I grew up in. I said I'd never come back the day I loaded up all of my stuff, yet here I am. I'd like to say it was me, but I know it was our baby. I wouldn't be here if it weren't for the hat of motherhood I'll put on sooner than later.

It's a small brick house, about thirteen hundred square feet of heated and cooled living space. It's a little bare since she never got into the whole 'making it a home' thing, like flower beds, porch furniture and door hangers, but for a single mother with no help I've always thought it was pretty nice.

I walk toward the steps, taking them one at a time. The front is elevated, as the house is sitting on somewhat of a slope. This wasn't exactly how I planned this, but after the conversation with Ella it needs to be done. A wave of nausea hits, but I breathe through it. My nerves are unsettled.

I ball up my fist and bring it toward the wood, beside the oval pane of glass in the center, preparing to knock, when the door opens. My mouth falls a little, and suddenly an empty feeling hits in the pit of my stomach. "Mom?"

The woman standing on the other side is someone I've never seen before. The woman I knew was strong-willed, hard, and well, a bitch. But she was also beautiful. The woman staring back at me is pale, frail, and her head is covered in a scarf. She looks tired, dark circles set deep beneath her eyes. She glances at my car in the driveway and then at me, before moving aside and waving me in.

I walk past her, glancing at her once more as I walk in, trying to confirm to myself that it's really her. Neither of us makes an attempt to speak. Despite the talk at Ella's and seeing her now, it's still hard to believe.

I stop in the center of the living room, looking around. It still looks the same as when I left it, only cleaner. A hint of lemon exists in the air. It smells of cleaning supplies and I swear I don't see one particle of dust. Other than that there is only one noticeable difference—photos of me along the timeline of my childhood sprinkled throughout the room; some in frames sitting on top of furniture, and others hung on the wall. I wasn't even aware she had this many pictures of me. I spot a few with a man I don't recognize flanking her side with his arm around her in each one. He looks a little older than her, which confuses me even more. Every man I've ever known her to date got younger with each one instead of older.

The door shuts, preceding the several moments of silence. "You have the pregnancy glow."

Following her familiar voice my eyes close, and my hand touches my stomach, before falling. I turn and look at her, trying to keep calm even though my nerves have a different idea, but my eyes settle on her worn-down expression and I stare. Who is this person? Her voice doesn't even match what I remember of her. She was always angry or annoyed, her voice hard. This version is peaceful, soft. "Is that why you're here?"

"I'm here for closure. It was just the push I needed to come."

The back door closing grabs my attention. "Leigh Anne . . . Cale will be here by six." Footsteps sound until the man from the photos appears in the doorway, speaking until he notices me. His eyes lock with mine, before he looks me over. He's clean-cut, his dark hair peppered with gray, eyes brown. He has kind eyes, a face lined with wisdom, and of an age that holds a lot of knowledge. He's handsome, in that older Gerard Butler kind of way. He smiles at me, never missing a beat. "You must be Delta," he says, catching me off guard.

"Yes. I wish I could return the recognition. Who are you?"

He walks toward me and pulls me into an embrace; the kind I would think a father does with his daughter. It's awkward, seemingly more for me. "My name is Jim. I'm your stepdad. It's great to finally meet you. Will you be staying for dinner? My son is coming home from medical school for the weekend." He nods toward one of the walls. "He'd love to meet the girl in the photos. I know I have been."

Everything in my head starts swarming. I step back, unable to process anything with the anger and confusion mixing inside of me. Everything feels normal, a decade or so too late. "I'm sorry, what?"

I look at her. Is that guilt on her face? Sadness? I'm not familiar with these expressions she's wearing; at least not coming from her. She takes a deep breath, her shoulders relaxing from the tensed position they were in, before coming over and giving him a hug. "Jim, darling, why don't you let Delta and I talk out back. We knew if this ever happened it was going to be complicated, and I'm tired. I need to sit."

He kisses her forehead. "Of course. I'll make two glasses of sweet tea and then head to the store for steaks." He glances back over at me. "You're welcome to stay as long as you'd like, Delta. We've been hoping for this day for quite a while. I'll pick up an extra ribeye, just in case, but there is no pressure to stay longer than you're comfortable."

And with that he walks into the kitchen. I'm in a state of shock. She doesn't make any effort to move closer to me, and for that I'm thankful. I walk toward the wall he was pointing at. It's a section holding my senior portrait, dressed out in my cap and gown. Beside me is a male in the same attire, only a different color. He's cute— slender but not skinny, dirty blonde hair only a shade lighter than brown, and the prettiest blue eyes I've ever seen. They're almost clear they're so light. I'm guessing that comes from his mother. To a stranger it'd look like a normal family, and that thought has me laughing inside.

I continue staring at my photo, remembering all too well the last time I wore that. I can almost feel the sting on my cheek where she slapped me and told me to get out of her house, and for me to never show my face around her again, because she no longer had a daughter. The memories rush back as if years don't separate us. Maybe I should have waited on Kross for this. The emotions are quickly becoming too much to sort through. "Maybe I shouldn't have come. You have a new family now."

She takes a step forward, but stops when I step back. "Delta, it's not like that. I know you're confused by everything you see, but there is a lot to say. I had hopes that you would show back up here one day, even though I was prepared for the opposite after the way we left things. You're already here. Let me explain over a glass of tea before I'm out of chances. Then, if you want to, you're free to leave."

"Tea? The mother I remember had more of a wine preference."

"I stopped drinking shortly after you left."

I can feel the slap all over again, even though a hand doesn't come flying. "You had a change of heart after that many years? But you never tried to contact me? You disowned me."

The tears fall before I can dismiss them. Hers gloss over shortly after. "I needed to fix myself first. Then, so much time went by. Jim happened and things recently changed with my health. I wasn't sure you wanted to see me. You didn't need the burden of my current state after everything. It would have been selfish."

"How did you even know I was okay, or alive for that matter?"

"When Katherine—God rest her soul—wasn't a walking liquor bottle or strung out on drugs I managed to get information out of her. I knew you were doing well in Atlanta. You girls really did okay for yourselves, despite everything. Please, let's go outside." I glance at the front door, deciding if I want to leave. "Delta, I may not live long enough to know I have a grandchild, please, just give me an hour."

More tears fall, remembering I'm no longer a child but soon to be a mother, and Ella's conversation comes back to me. Her opinion is one of the few that matters, and she asked me to give her a shot. "Okay."

She leads me through the same but slightly different kitchen, grabbing both glasses of tea off the island, handing me a Mason jar with a lemon slice wedged on the rim. I take it and follow her out the back door. The patio has been turned into an enclosed sunroom overlooking the backyard, but the electric fireplace freestanding in the corner is keeping it warm.

She sits in one of two wicker chairs, setting her glass of tea on the small table that separates us. She makes use of the matching ottoman by propping her feet up as I take the other. Surprisingly, it's more comfortable than it looks. I take a sip of the tea as she settles, pulling a blanket off the back of her chair and draping it over her lap. I've forgotten how good home brewed tea is versus restaurant quality. "Do you need a blanket?"

"No. It's warm in here."

"When are you due?"

"The end of July."

"I don't see a ring. Is there a special someone?"

"Yes."

"Will there be a wedding?"

"He's not the marrying kind. It's fine. I don't need a piece of paper to prove that he loves me."

"I see."

"Is this what this is going to be? Small talk. It's weird. We've never sat around and had mother daughter bonding time."

"I suppose I deserve that."

The air becomes thick from the awkward silence. I take another sip, trying to busy myself. "Just so we're clear, Chuck wasn't your fault. It was mine."

And there it is. The icebreaker. I turn toward her, eyes downcast on my hands from the shame, pulling one leg into the seat. More tears fall. "I could have said no," I whisper, finally admitting my own mistakes. "I was lonely and selfishly seeking attention. I was angry with you."

"I know." I look at her, eying the tear trails down her cheeks. "We're never going to move forward if we don't clear the air. If you're anything like me you're tired of the bitterness, of the anger, of the resentment. I've been praying for this opportunity for a long time, and here you are. The final step of my recovery is mending broken bridges; seeking forgiveness from those I've wronged."

"Recovery?"

"Yes, recovery. The day of your graduation when Chuck pledged his love for you and said he was leaving me, I got angry. By the time you found me after the ceremony I was in the spiral downward. I was so angry all I could do was react. And I'm sorry that you saw me at my worst. I wasn't even really angry with you, Delta. I was angry with myself. You were a child. I was suddenly living in every single mother's worst nightmare. I'm not saying you didn't make bad decisions, but it's not like I was that great of a role model for you either. When I was finally alone and honest with myself it was no shock. I saw the way he looked at you on more than one occasion. There were times when I woke up to him getting back in bed with a certain smell I knew didn't come from watching television. Deep down I think I knew something was going on between you two. Instead of being the parent I drowned myself in my wine, in nightlife, and in work. What happened was my fault because I left you at home with my boyfriends over the years. I trusted too freely. The two of you spent a lot of time here together. I overlooked things that should have never been overlooked. A lot of things now make sense, looking back. It's all on me. I was supposed to be your mother, not your roommate or your friend. I should have never said those things to you. And I most certainly should have never laid my hand on you that way."

"It wasn't really anything different than what you've said or done over the years."

She wipes her face as a new set of tears fall. "You're right. I was a horrible mother. There is no excuse that could make how I treated you okay, but I do owe you an explanation. Especially now that you're an adult. I was recently diagnosed with stage four cervical cancer. It's also in my ovaries and uterus. I'm prepared to fight. I'm undergoing necessary care and treatment, but with cancer there is a very real possibility that I could die. I've made peace with most things, but I can't fathom the thought of leaving this world without at least trying to make amends with you. You're my only child. Regardless of anything I've ever made you think I love you. I was young when I got pregnant with you, much younger than you are. What I thought was a fun, spontaneous weekend ended up having permanent consequences. I have no idea what your father's name is or where he lives; nothing more than an old image in my head of him that fades a little more with every year that passes. I snuck out that morning thinking I was taking away a memory with a soldier. Six weeks later I got two pink lines and a write off from my parents that I've tried to fix many times. They want nothing to do with me. I ended up alone and bitter, broke, with a baby thrown in the mix that depended on me. I worked my way up from the first job I could get that paid a salary that was worth a damn without a college degree.

My friends left me. I missed out on college. Dating became a game to hold onto my youth. With every hurdle I jumped the depression got worse. I turned to alcohol and took any overtime offered. I was a functioning addict between wine and men. I became emotionally distant. Then, you got older and started adopting this darker style I didn't understand—the tattoos, the revealing clothing, the black. I didn't know how to connect with you. You're beautiful, Delta. God, if you could only see it. You took everything I said to heart, but I was too far-gone to care. So many times I've sat and wondered how the hell I created such a beautiful child. The older you got and the more your body matured the more you reminded me of myself all those years ago, and what I missed out on because I was saddled with a child. I lashed out at you. What I needed was a therapist to deal with things I'd let build for years."

Her face is soaked. I'm dying inside. My heart is pounding so hard it's taking more effort to breathe. I've never once in my entire life seen her this emotional. Her voice cracks every few sentences. "It wasn't until you packed your things and left that I realized how wrong I was. Even though I threatened it I didn't expect you to leave. But you did. And everything became obvious—I had a problem. For years I thought of how much easier it would be without someone depending on me, then you left and the house was deafening. It was maddening. My drinking got worse. There was a stretch where I had a new man in my bed nightly, most of which I brought home from Ella's. I called in to work instead of getting out of bed. I almost lost my job. When I found out that you were taking bartending classes something snapped. I realized I had done exactly what I thought I wanted. I taught you to be strong, to not need anyone, especially a man or me. I was finally free, but with that freedom came a gaping hole in my chest. I took a leave of absence and checked myself into rehab. I found healing, spirituality, meditation. I even learned to forgive myself, but the one thing that was still missing was you."

"Then why didn't you come find me? I'm supposed to just believe you turned over a new leaf, yet you didn't have the decency to try and fix it? Not even in the midst of you getting fucking married! It doesn't seem like you've missed me at all. In the end I'm still the one that came here! I spent years chasing your love, but for once you couldn't chase mine? I missed out on my own childhood, Mom. Did you know Chuck fucked me seven ways to Sunday while you were in the next room, awake a lot of those times? He got off on knowing you could catch us, and because I was so starved for attention I let him. I even let him knowing he was still fucking you. How fucked up must I be to have been screwing the same man as my mother? And that's not even the best part. He recruited me as a minor to strip in his club. Promised me things —like I would have money for myself, money that you weren't giving me because you were selfish. I was bound by secrets. Prepped to act older than I was. I was lying to you so that we could be together for weekends at a time in the house he would never take you to. In your own warped little world you either didn't care or didn't notice. That day I walked away from you both, but if you had given a damn to come see for yourself you'd know that I wasn't doing well. I was living paycheck to paycheck, even when things were great. In the end it wasn't even as easy as in the beginning. Because I prioritized a dream I had for myself I was well on my way to being homeless. Instead of drowning in pity at how broke I had become, or going to my mom for help like most girls would have done, I went back to Chuck and asked him for my job back."

Tears I didn't know I was holding back spill with no shame. "He gave it back to me, but it wasn't without a cost. All the filth I felt when I was in high school came back full force and then some, but this time it didn't just last for the fifteen minutes it took him to get off. No, I felt like a whore for a long time after. Honestly I think it was worse, because I had bettered myself. I had more choices than before, and I had proven that I was capable of doing it on my own. Even still, it wasn't bad enough for me to treat the ones around me like shit. I never forced the people I care about to carry my cross. So forgive me if it's a little difficult for me to believe you. It's going to take a lot more than a few tears and cancer for me to just forget everything that easily."

She buries her face in her hands, her cries louder than before. I stand and walk to one of the windows, staring outside at a view I'm all too familiar with, contemplating leaving. "Please tell me he's not the father," she whispers. "I'm not sure if I'd be able to forgive myself for that."

The desperation in her voice sends a crack traveling down my heart like a rock hitting a windshield with a lot of force. "No. I was at least smart enough not to let that bastard knock me up. The man that did is an all-consuming asshole that demands his own way, has no filter of appropriate things to say, and evokes every emotion in a matter of minutes. He steals everyone's focus by merely walking in a room. He's talented. He's a man of few words. And he's an alpha to the core. But he's also been through far worse things than either you or I. His name is Kross. I'm completely and inevitably in love with him."

"He sounds like a lucky man."

"No, I'm the lucky one."

"I'm so sorry, Delta. You're right. I should have come, but I wanted to be a better person for you. I wanted to love myself first or I knew I wouldn't be able to love you like you deserve. When I was finally becoming a better person —reasonably happy with myself—I met Jim in a small group at the church I started visiting. We hit it off. He's taught me so much about life, love, and laughter . . . Then I was diagnosed with cancer and everything has been a whirlwind ever since. I didn't think you'd want to see me, so I waited, because I knew if you showed back up here then your heart was far bigger than mine and there was hope that I could earn your forgiveness after all."

A small bird perches on the branch of the oak in the backyard— the one that she carved our names in when I was five. I remember that day so clearly, as if it was yesterday. It was the middle of spring; the perfect temperature and the wild flowers were in bloom. I wanted to play outside in the sunshine. I begged her all morning. She had been cleaning the majority of it. Had my room spic and span before I asked for the final time so that she wouldn't say no. She was sitting at the kitchen table, sorting out and paying bills like she did once a month; at least that's what she always said she was doing. I was five. I didn't understand more than the words coming out of her mouth.

When she looked up at me holding the Dust Buster—because let's face it, I was much too little to operate a full sized vacuum— she took off her glasses with a smile on her face and stood up. I think her exact words were, "Any girl that can help her mommy by cleaning her own room deserves a little fun." And then she picked me up and off we went. Days like that was the reason I tried so hard.

I can hear the screams of joy in my head from her pushing me on the tire swing she still has hanging from that branch she put up when she had her tires changed on her car that year. It should have been an old truck tire, but when it's just two girls you make do with what you've got. It fit me perfectly back then.

I wipe my eyes to clear my vision. "Why didn't you take it down?"

I tense when she puts her arm around me, not even realizing she had gotten up. She's so scrawny now. "We had a lot of good times on that old thing. I think it has a lot left in it yet. I'd like to be able to push my grandchild on it too."

"Mom, don't—"

"Delta, I'm not asking you to trust me. Once destroyed I know that's not something that can easily be fixed. I'm not even asking you to decide right now. All I'm asking you is to give me a chance to show you I'm serious, to show you I'm sorry and want us to build a relationship. If I'm successful then maybe you can consider letting me be a part of your child's life, and your special someone. Kross, is it?"

Again, Ella's conversation is hitting me hard. She kept saying she's changed. To listen to her. To lay down my anger and open my heart. Then I remember how Lux looked when her mother died. It didn't matter how shitty the woman was she still lost it. She still grieved the loss. The good times triumphed over the bad. And now she's out of chances. Maybe I'm too forgiving. Or maybe I'm too easy to crack, but either way, I don't think those are qualities that I'd be disappointed to pass down to my child.

I can't help but wonder—if Lux had the chance to change things with her mother before she died would she forgive everything in the past to try for a different future? It's already been answered. Of course she would. She moved the woman into her apartment with her, despite everything that she knew she was; even with the possibility that she would never change.

I turn toward her, leaning my shoulder against the glass, and then the dam breaks as the words expel from my mouth. "And if you make me love you again and you die. Then what?"

She cups my face with her frail hands, wiping the tears away as she lets hers run down her face. "Then you finish out your life with better memories of me and I die in peace. That's the best thing I could hope for."

With the sincerity in her voice I know I'm going to cave. I'm tired of coping with the loss of her. And I'm just tired. I've been angry for a long time. It's exhausting. It's time for me to grow up, to practice being the mother I want to be. "Fine, but if you let me down I swear to God I'm done."

She pulls my head against her chest, and for a moment we cry together, before I finally gather my wits and pull away, wiping at my face and clearing my throat. "So, tell me about Jim."

She lights up in a way I've never seen in regards to a man and leads me back to the chairs we were previously sitting in. "Tea, we're going to need a lot more tea . . ."

For once, tea sounds a hell of a lot better than wine.

I walk out back, past the sunroom to the familiar sounds of the outdoors, needing a little bit of fresh air. It has been a busy day, and the exhaustion is hitting hard. Today Mom and I talked more than we have my entire life. It's a little surreal, but it was nice. I'm trying to tell myself not to freak out over everything, but the second I'm back home I probably will. At the moment I haven't had a chance to think.

A walkway of pavers that I don't recognize leads to a swing. It's inviting, the way the solar lights navigate you from point A to point

B. I follow the brick road toward it and take a seat, allowing my back to conform against the wood planks. I zip up my warm jacket and place my hands inside the pockets, before leaning my head back.

I close my eyes, listening to the dogs barking down the street along with a few kids yelling, probably being told to come inside out of the cold. Right now it doesn't seem like it has any advantages over the city, but in the summer it's hard to beat. I've spent many warm summer nights sitting outside, smoking with the radio down low, listening to the crickets ramble while I watched the lightning bugs show their asses; literally. I was always a little fond of country life, though I would have never admitted it. It has a certain peace that you can't get anywhere else.

It's amazing to me that you can have all this and then drive a couple hours down the highway and you're in a place like Atlanta; a great big city that never slows down, never enjoys the sounds of nature, and certainly never sleeps. It's like two different worlds existing beside each other.

I open my eyes, the black sky saying hello, glittering with its own version of diamonds. I wish Kross were here to see this. I think he'd appreciate the quiet. I push off with my feet, before picking them up as the swing moves back and forth, my hair swishing along with the movement. I haven't done this in a long time. "Mind if I sit?"

I stop the swing with my feet, glancing up at the additional body now standing a few feet away in slim-fitting jeans and a long sleeved thermal, beneath a jacket. His hair is gelled in a way I think it's supposed to look blow-dried. "You are aware that you look like a Hollister model, right?"

He laughs, before taking a seat beside me. "So I've been told. Well, model that is. I don't think anyone has ever been quite that specific. Though, to be honest, I'm not sure that's the whole vibe I'm going for if I want my patients to call me Dr. Andrews and actually take me seriously."

"Might wanna tone down that whole surfer boy hairdo you have going on then. What's up, Cale?"

"How weird is it that you're no longer an only child?"

"I'm not completely sure I'm not lost in a twilight zone."

"I can imagine since you weren't here for the wedding and all. It must be strange walking into all this. It was awkward for me and I had more time to adjust."

A small ache in my chest catches my attention with the reminder. "Definitely not what I was expecting."

"If it makes you feel better, she talked about you all the time. She told us things. Hard to believe some of the stuff she said."

"How about we start off with lighter conversation before hitting the hard stuff? I'm all tapped out on emotional for today."

"Very well then. So you're a tattoo artist?"

"In training."

He smiles at me. "What?"

"How does a girl that looks like you get into that line of work?"

"I like to draw. I like tattoos even more. Why is that so surprising to people?"

He shrugs. "Just is. You strike me as more of a tattoo model than the artist. How many tattoos do you have anyway? You can't really see anything with all of the winter clothes. If it wasn't for the lip rings I'd say you look completely normal."

"Maybe because I am normal . . . And I didn't know an artist had a certain look," I say, aggravated. "Not counting my sleeves in progress—my arms are close to being covered—I have eight, but it's only a matter of time till I have more."

"Can I see? I've never personally known a girl with that many tattoos. That was frowned upon at the private school I went to. If you had them they weren't allowed to show."

"Only if you want my boyfriend to beat you to death before you ever get that doctorate degree. He doesn't look as normal as me," I tease.

"Okay then . . ."

An awkward silence lingers. I nudge his shoulder. "But in the spring or summer a lot of them will be on display. Maybe then."

He smiles again. "Good to know you'll be around. It sucks being a third wheel with those two in there."

"So you're a doctor?"

"In training," he says, a playful smirk on his face.

"How does a guy that looks like you get into that line of work?" I repeat back his question sarcastically.

"My little brother died from Leukemia at the age of four."

My mouth drops. "I-I-Fuck, I'm sorry. I didn't know."

"It's fine. I didn't expect you to."

"So you're going into . . ."

"Pediatric Oncology."

"Wow. That's honorable. Do you think you'll be able to handle that daily? I can't imagine what they must see and deal with."

"Someone has to. If everyone looked at it from the point that kids are dying there'd never be anyone to save them. I'm not saying it'll be easy, but to save a life from ending before it's truly had a chance to live will make the rest worth it." He places his arm on the back of the swing behind me. I look at it. "I'm your brother, Delta. Mind out of the gutter. It's harmless," he teases.

"Stepbrother. I've heard of worse things happening. You just better be glad my boyfriend isn't here to see this shit."

"That never crossed my mind, but if I was going to tap into a taboo

fantasy I'm glad you look like that. It could be our little secret . . ."
He pulls me closer for effect, before laughing and removing his arm. I
shove his head away, laughing along with him. He definitely takes the
tension out of the room easily. I figured that out around an awkwardly
silent dinner table earlier when he started talking about crap at school
that was way over my head.

He leans over, forearms to thighs, and looks out in front of us.
Everything becomes silent, like it was before, the two of us existing
without interacting. But something occurs to me now that we're
alone and it's appropriate conversation. "Where is your mom?"

"I thought we weren't getting heavy."

"Okay, fine. One for one."

"After my brother died she couldn't deal. Took off. It's just been
Dad and me since. Well, till your mom. She makes him happier.
She gives him company, especially now that I'm away at college all
the time. Since I got into medical school it's not as easy to make the
drive home."

"How old were you?"

"Six."

"So she lost one child but abandoned the other?"

He shrugs again. "I guess if that's the way you want to look at
it. Can't say I blame her. My brother was almost an exact carbon
copy of me, only two years younger. Everyone used to comment
about how we missed being identical twins, even after he was gone.
I reminded her of him. They say the loss of a child is like no other
type of loss. It changes people. No clue where she even is. I just
hope she found peace. I had enough with Dad. I'm not angry at
her."

"I wish I had your outlook on life."

"My turn." I turn and look at him, waiting. "What's the real reason you and your mom haven't spoken in years? Some of the stuff she says just doesn't add up. At least it doesn't seem like a bad enough reason to never speak or see each other. If my mom came back and wanted a relationship I would take it in a heartbeat, regardless of what she did or who she wronged. Life is too short to hold on to anger when it means cutting family out of your life."

"It's not really something I want to talk about. I don't need your judgment. I barely know you."

"I would never judge you. I'm trying to understand."

"We had a strained relationship. I grew up without a father, and a mostly absent mother. I was alone a lot, and because of that I learned to crave the wrong kind of attention. I was starved for physical touch, for intimacy, so the first person that gave it to me I took it openly."

"What am I missing?"

God, I didn't realize just how shameful it was until I was forced to be open about it. Secrets don't seem that bad when you're the only one that knows about them. And Lux, but she doesn't count. We know all of each other's secrets. I take a deep breath, my nerves attempting to get the best of me. I could never be Catholic. I don't like this whole confessional thing. "That person was my mom's boyfriend. We had a lengthy affair, until he told her he was leaving her for me the day of my high school graduation, without my consent. She sent me away."

The air is stifling. "That would definitely put a damper on things," he says, before everything becomes silent. The embarrassment slices through me like a knife cutting into butter. I never felt like this with Kross. Since day one we have been everything the other needed. The best part is that it comes naturally. He had a way of accepting everything about me, good and bad, without making me

144

feel like a goddamned whore waiting to be stoned, and he's said some pretty harsh things.

I stand, preparing to walk back inside and say my goodbyes. He grabs my hand, pulling me back down into the seat. "I was thinking, not judging."

"Thinking about?"

"That this friendship could work out in our favor. Confession is the spiritual cleansing of the soul. You could confide in me, and me in you. And because we don't know anything about each other's personal lives no one else gets hurt."

"I'm not following."

"I need some advice. But it, too, would be frowned upon to anyone else. After that, I know you would understand. I had a feeling about you from the moment I arrived, but I needed to know what that feeling was first. I needed to know that I could trust you."

"I'm fine not knowing. Prefer it really. This doesn't have to be a tit for tat kind of thing. What part of *I'm fucked up* did you not read between the lines. I hardly think I qualify to give someone advice."

He turns and looks behind him at the house, his eyes skittering from window to window, then to the door. "What are you doing? You're freaking me out. If you're going to admit that you're an ax murderer in your spare time I know people that are worse. Choose your victim wisely."

He glances at me, his hand gripped on the back of the swing, a smile touching his eyes but not showing on his lips. "Why do I feel like that's not really a joke?"

The center of my brow hits twelve o'clock. "Maybe I am, maybe I'm not, but is that something you'd really want to risk finding out? On with it. At some point this baby I'm incubating is going to request the heat and my boyfriend is going to psycho stalk me if I don't get back to my phone within a reasonable time frame."

He rubs his hands down his face. "Shit. I'm sleeping with my best friend's fiancé. It happened after a late night study session one night and has continued. The bad part is we're fucking crazy about each other. We can't stop the madness. And now I don't think I want to. I don't know what to do."

I smack his shoulder. "Way to rip off the 'welcome to the family' Band-Aid, Cale! Fuck, you could've warned me."

"I've been living with this secret for months. It's slowly destroying me. I can't focus on my classes half the time. I'm taking time away from studying so that we can meet in secret. I need this to end, but either way I'm going to lose someone."

"If you are meant to be with someone honesty is the most natural part of the relationship. When I'm around Kross I develop diarrhea of the mouth and everything comes out. I mean, maybe you're doing your best friend a favor. If she's cheating on him with you then clearly she doesn't need to get married. And if the two of you are really in love then maybe he'll understand and be supportive. Just talk to him. Y'all should come clean before you get caught and it's worse."

He's biting his lip, trying to hold back a laugh. "Why are you laughing? I told you I was shit at advice but I hardly think this is funny."

"Delta."

"What?"

"Sarah is my best friend. Her fiancé is Troy."

Understanding slides into place and my mouth makes an O as the drawn out form of the word exits behind it. "I got nothin'."

"How would you feel?"

"Well, first I would cut his dick off for cheating instead of coming to me. We're all adults. I would rather have a chance to move on myself than to look like a fool in front of everyone."

"Fuck. I knew we should have stopped after the first time until we could figure things out, but it was so much better than I ever thought it'd be."

"Whoa, no. No details."

"Sorry. This is what he does to me! I can't focus!"

"Have you always been?"

"No. We're each other's firsts. Always been with females in the past. It's great, but this is something else entirely. I think I'm in love with him."

"Well . . . I can certainly see the appeal with cock, obviously, and especially with the right person or baby B wouldn't be in existence. It's great. BUT. You need to tell her. God, I've always thought that'd be a girl's worst nightmare—for a man to leave her for another man. At least if it's a woman there is some form of competition. Talk about something that could deflate your ego and destroy your sexual self-esteem . . ."

"I don't want to hurt her. We met at State freshman year. She's important to me. If we hadn't hit it off so well as friends I would have tried to date her."

"Oh, I think it's safe to say that ship has sailed if she loved him enough to say yes. Cheating scenarios are never going to end happily. The good news is forgiveness is a powerful tool. Kind of why I'm still here," I mumble.

"I guess you're right."

"You two are going to catch a cold. If you're going to stay outside at least build a fire for her, Cale. Where are your manners?"

We glance back at the same time to Jim hanging out the door. "Okay, Dad. I think we're about to come inside."

I yawn as he shuts the door, remembering I still have a long drive ahead of me. "I think that's my cue to go. I still have to drive back to Atlanta and it's getting late."

He follows behind me as I stand. "Hey, Delta? Mind keeping this between us? I need to permanently sort things out before I talk to Dad. He has certain . . . beliefs. Something like that I can't take back."

"Not my secret to tell, Cale. We all have them. The good thing about secrets is that you choose who gets to be a part of them."

I begin walking toward the house. He keeps pace, but before we get to the door he nudges my shoulder like earlier. "I think I'm going to like having a sister."

And me—I think I'm going to like having a family . . .

CHAPTER FOURTEEN

Kross

Twenty-eight days I've been following his every move. Twenty-seven nights I've spent away from my bed, without my girl. I miss her. All of her. I miss her attitude when she's aggravated at me—and recently that's been a lot over my absence. I miss her bitchiness of what I'm assuming is just part of being a girl. And I miss the way she wants to fucking touch me all the time. I must admit it's a strange feeling to be here, in the sense of wanting a woman this way, of wanting to be touched. I never thought I'd experience this, but now that I'm here, I'll kill before I'll let it go. God knows I check her location every few hours, and it's not because I don't trust her. It's because I don't trust anyone else.

I hold my binoculars to my eyes, watching as his car pulls up to the back entrance of the strip club. I glance at my watch. Right on time, just as I expected. I've stayed out of sight, watching him from a distance; mapping out his behavior, memorizing his schedule, and plotting his death. I've done my homework. I've studied the motherfucker real hard. I've put in the time. I've been patient, but my patience is wearing thin. I had planned for this to be a quick job. I figured out that was a little presumptuous 14 days in. He's careful, he's precise, and he knows how to cover his ass, never going anywhere without two human versions of the hulk. It would be so easy to take him out right here while I have him in my sights. If only the binoculars were my scope. I have a sniper rifle for the perfect head shot, but instead, I'll wait a little more, because I want him to know the bastard that took him out—the bastard he created.

A sadistic laugh fills the cab of the truck. Fucking bodyguards. I guess he's not as tough with a little age on him. A rush of anger floods my soul, feeding it as I watch him enter, dressed out in a dark suit. Just as the door opens I get a glimpse of that cross on his neck, and every time I do the memories take over. They come regular and stronger now, as if all they needed was the right key to unlock them. It looks exactly the same, only faded compared to all those years ago when I first saw it.

He disappears inside, distantly sandwiched between the two goons. My sanity is on the verge of breaking if I don't get back to her soon, and that's something I've meticulously controlled my entire life. My phone starts to vibrate on the center console of the rental. I glance at it, deciding if I want to let it go to voicemail and call her back later. I'm so close. I have a plan. Tonight is the night. Then I can go home. Before I have a chance to decide the phone is already at my ear. "Delta. What is it?"

"I know I'm not supposed to call you first . . ." Her voice cracks, the sniffles into the phone putting me on high alert. She sounds like she's crying. Why the fuck is she crying?

"What's wrong? Did someone hurt you?"

"I know the sex of the baby."

I blink over and over, zoned out, trying to understand what she's saying. "What do you mean?"

She sighs and takes a deep breath. "Kross, I told you about the appointment two weeks ago. You were supposed to come home in time for it."

Christ. I stare straight ahead, every thought in my head racing. A feeling I don't recognize slams into the forefront of my mind. "Why didn't you reschedule and wait for me? You know I'm on a job. An important one."

"I could have had it done as early as sixteen weeks. I have waited. You never called. I assumed you didn't care."

"Why didn't you fucking remind me?"

"Because you're off chasing the ghost of Kross' past," she cries into the phone. "Why can't you let it go? I came home just like you wanted. I've waited a month since you left. I've slept alone in our bed. I feel like an intruder in your house without you here. I miss you."

"It's your damn house too, Delta. I'll be home as soon as this is done."

"Is this how it's going to be? You putting things that no longer matter before me? It's fucking ironic that the woman I've despised for years has contacted me daily attempting to build a relationship while the man that fathered my child is acting like I'm an afterthought. I have to go somewhere you aren't expecting me to be for you to call me. Well, I'm getting tired of it. I gave you the option to be single and you chose for us to be together. I'm lonely and you don't even care. I've basically spent my entire life being alone. I can't take it anymore. I just wanted to let you know I'm turning my phone off for a while. I stare at it constantly, waiting for you to call or text. It's pathetic and old at this point. I need a break. You want to talk to me then you can come home. Oh, and it's a fucking girl."

She disconnects the call, leaving me in some kind of warped space-time continuum. Thoughts begin piecing together like a puzzle. A girl? A female. Lack of dick and balls. Pussy present. I'm going to have a . . . daughter? That was hardly what I expected. The vision of him fucking that fifteen-year-old comes back. I remember that Delta was fucking a grown man as a teenager. That same grown man. "Motherfucker." I slam my fists into the steering wheel. "As if I'm not enough of a goddamned psycho." A boy I think I could handle. But a girl . . . Too many people are likely to die. And killing teenage kids is not my thing.

My head falls against the headrest. The screen of my phone lights up, signaling a video message has been received. I open the message from Delta, tapping the play button. It looks just like that first ultrasound photo I found under the mattress, only different. My eyes hone in to the creature in the center that looks oddly like a skeleton. Hands, arms, and knees . . . It's moving. The video isn't long, only about ten to fifteen seconds. A photo comes in right after it ends. I'm not even sure what I'm looking at with it being black and gray scale, but the text out beside it is idiot-proof. "I'm a girl!"

I call her. It rings several times before going to her voicemail. I hang up and call again. Three more times I call before she finally answers. "You don't give up, do you?"

"It's a girl. We have a daughter?"

Her breathing evens out. "Yeah, Kross, we have a daughter."

I fist my hair, trying to work through the questions in my head. Trying to find the words. "Is she okay? Does she have the right number of toes and shit?"

One laugh slips through the phone, but nothing else follows. "Yeah, baby, she's perfect."

"Anyone else know?"

"No. Despite your absence I wanted you to be the first."

"Not even Lux?"

"Lux is my best friend. But that doesn't mean she's entitled to this kind of information before you. This is ours."

"Does she have a name?"

"No. Why would I name her without you?"

"Why would you name her with me? I remember promising you I'd be there now. I'm an asshole. I wouldn't have been mad."

Her exhale sounds through the phone. "Kross, I'm not clueless. I knew what I was getting into with you. I was hurt you didn't come, although not completely surprised, but that doesn't mean I want to do those things without you. She's our daughter. We name her together."

"She needs a name."

"She does. I can wait till you come home. We have time."

"No. She needs a name. We aren't calling her a thing."

"You want to name her over the phone?"

"I got time to kill."

"I'd rather you come home."

I rub my jaw. "I'll be home tomorrow."

"Don't feed me false hope."

"You have my word."

"I like the name Emery. It means powerful, ruler of work, brave. I figure she needs a strong name with parents like us."

I stare at that building, knowing this is going to be over soon, one way or another. I failed at protecting her—the woman that gave birth to me. She protected me. A scared shitless little boy, I stood there. A failure that won't happen twice. Murder is a skill I'm good at. Hunting is a game I like. To kill is a high that doesn't exist in any drug. It gives you a sense of power that can't be earned any other way. A human with no conscience is a lethal being. It edges on the line of immortality. Delta thinks I care. I choose not to correct her. She has no idea the demons that drive me. The only thing I've ever cared about is her. Arms dealing and tattooing are things I found to keep me at peace; to satiate the fucked-up desires I carry inside. It gives me a sense of normalcy. They made me this way; they gave me my first tastes of death—him and that cunt that fostered me the longest. I never say her name, because a cunt is what she was. Delta and Emery are the two I have to protect. They'll be safe once he's gone. "I like Emery."

"Just like that? No catch? No alternatives? I was hardly expecting this to be simple."

"It fits."

"What about a middle name?"

"What's yours again?"

"Lynn."

"Go with that."

"But don't you want to pick?"

"I just did."

"But it's after me."

"You're her mother. Good ones are important. We should know."

"So are fathers . . ."

"She'll have it different than us."

"Promise?"

"Yes."

"If she's going to have something after me what can she have after you?"

"My last name. Even though it's not one of value or worth being passed down, it's the one she gave me. That has to mean something."

"Kross," she whispers, a sudden change in tone that resembles the one she had when she first called. "I never even considered giving her my last name. I would never take that from you."

"So it's settled then?"

"If you're sure it's what you want."

"I'm sure that's what it's supposed to be. That's the part that matters."

It gets quiet for a moment. I glance at my watch. Almost time to do this. "You're going to have to buy more cologne," she says, randomly.

"Why?"

"I used it all on your side of the bed. It's cold now. Hard to sleep. It helps, but it's lonely without you in bed. I hate it. Kross, I hate being without you. I just want you to know that no man has owned me before you. I've somehow lost myself, but also found me too. I need you to keep your promise this time. I need you to come home tomorrow."

"Stop worrying. It's not good for your body in that state." She sniffles again. "Are you working at the shop tonight?"

"No. I took off for the appointment. I'm at home in bed watching T.V."

I don't like this unsure, paranoid version of her. I need her happy, stress free, and by the sounds of it Remington is doing a shit job. "Do me a favor."

"What?"

"You still got the credit cards?"

"Yeah. I haven't used them."

"Why? I've been gone a long time. Have you used the cash?"

"No, I put it up. And because it makes me uncomfortable. They're yours; all of it—the money, the house . . ."

"Fuck, Delta. I gave those things to you for you to use. That makes them yours."

"That's just the way I am. I've always paid my own way. I'm not Lux. It's not like I'm your wife. I'm your girlfriend."

Wife? One of those things that make someone completely yours. I may see the perks now. "Is that something you'd want to be?"

"What?"

A second call starts coming through—Johnny. "Never mind, look, I need you to do something for me. Take the motherfucking credit cards or the cash—I don't give a shit which—and stock the house with food. Then I want you to go do girl shit all damn day. Hair, nails, shopping for you or baby stuff, get a massage—what makes no difference to me. I don't need you thinking about the stuff I'm doing. I'll be home by midnight. If it makes you uncomfortable to spend my money, then for fuck's sake, take Lux for physical support. I guarantee she won't be as modest with Kaston's."

"I don't . . . I can't. I'd want to pay you back. It'd hang over my head."

"You're going to pay me back in pussy when I get home. An entire month's worth. After a sex life with you and this kind of break my nuts feel like they're going to explode. Now shut the fuck up about it and do it. It's not optional at this point. I need to focus on the job so I can keep my promise. I can't miss my shot."

"Sometimes I want to kick you in the balls when you're a demanding asshole. If they weren't so useful to me I probably would."

It starts beeping in my ear again, Johnny trying to call through since I missed the first one. "I gotta go. I'll be busy from now until the time I get home. I need you to follow orders."

I switch over the call. "You got it?"

"Yeah, Man. Waiting on you."

"Meet me at the coordinates I sent in an hour. He should be here till close. I've seen extra girls filtering through. My guess is he's got a full house tonight. Even better for us."

"See you there."

I toss the phone down, adrenaline already building and spreading through my veins. It's time to get everything ready. This day has been coming for a long-ass time.

CHAPTER FIFTEEN
Kross

I t's a little after 3AM—go time. The clock is ticking on how much darkness I have left. I have to work fast. Daylight reveals too much—the time when the innocent come out of hiding and cops grow back their balls. Those of us that fear no evil prefer to walk at night.

The limo is parked in the alley beside the club, the driver standing against the side with a smoke in his mouth. I peek around the corner, waiting for him to turn his back on me. Upon the last drag he stomps out the bud, looking down at the pavement. I move quickly up behind him. The closer I get his head starts to turn. "Hey, who are—"

I stab the needle in his neck, injecting the horse tranquilizer into his muscle. Merely seconds pass and he's limp in my arms. I confiscate his chauffeur cap and badge, before removing his wallet from the pocket of his suit, ridding it of all cash and then tossing the rest to make it look like an amateur robbery. I drag his ass down the alley, rounding the corner to the back dumpster used by the strip club. I toss him inside, closing the lid. He'll be out for a while.

I grab my suit jacket nearby, pulling it on. Grabbing each lapel I secure the button properly and then I quickly clip the badge into place to be seen. I take the cap and pull it on my head, forcing it low so that it covers my eyes. The rest Johnny brought me earlier to ensure it was the right size so that I have no problems looking the part.

Closing my eyes, I take a deep breath, preparing myself for a kill, and savoring the excitement before the rush is gone. It's time to fucking do this.

I walk toward the car and take my place beside the back door, waiting. Ten minutes of being still in the dead of night and the door to the club opens. He exits, alone, barking orders into his phone— the only time of day I've seen him without his bodyguards since I started following him. My heart starts pounding against my chest with each step he takes toward me, remembering the last time he was this close. And with each foot he gains the anger turns into fuel. I breathe steady to keep calm as I open the back door, staying quiet, letting him enter with my head down.

As he successfully reaches the inside of the car I shut the door, feeling nothing but utter bliss inside as I make my way to the driver's door, getting in. I ask no questions, as his driver already knows exactly where he's supposed to go. I play the part down to the letter.

Step one down: secure the target.

Step two underway: in transit to kill zone.

I've researched everything there is to know about this city. One of the greatest skills to possess as a killer is a photographic memory. I know every field location, every low-key piece of land surrounded by trees, and every body of water within a hundred mile radius. I've marked sewer holes on the map in my head, including abandoned buildings and construction zones.

The window between us remains closed, giving him his privacy, and with slow and steady effort I pull the car out onto the road. On the way to the final destination I relive every moment I've seen him in my head, starting with the first time, the time that would always cut off in my dreams, before I remembered everything . . .

I follow behind him through the dark room, the one that has all the pretty, bright-colored lights on the walls. He pulls on my arm, making me walk faster than my short legs can go. It hurts. "Ow," I call out, tears making my face wet.

"Come, on, boy," he says in a voice that scares me. Rachel's is always soft. She's nice to me. I have to call her Rachel unless we're at home. She said it's to keep me safe.

"You're hurting me!"

He stops at a door and turns around. The back of his hand knocks me into the wall, my bones hurting as I try to stand up. I scream out in pain. I don't want to be here anymore. "Keep talking, you little shit, and I'll show you what real pain is."

He grabs the top of my arm and pulls me inside when he pushes the door open. It's an office. That much I know. This must be the place Mama said people go to get in trouble by the boss. I'm supposed to always stay where I'm told so that we don't end up having to go there. "Elliot, let him go! It's not what you think."

"Mama?" I close my eyes and hit myself against my head with my fist. "Stupid, stupid," I whisper.

I fight to turn around, but his nails are digging into my skin.

I want to see her. I want to go home. She runs down the hall, her clothes still missing. He grabs her by the throat. "No! Please don't hurt my Rachel."

"Not what I think, huh? Do you just have random little boys calling you 'Mama'?"

"He belongs to a friend," she says. "She's bad off on drugs. I'm just looking after him for a while."

He laughs, squeezing onto her neck tighter, causing her to gulp for air while her fingers dig into his hands. He turns his head to look at me, the colors of the painting on his neck moving. Mama taught me it's a cross. That it's important when we pray. He pulls her into the room and slams the door, locking it. "You must think I'm stupid, bitch. Funny how much your friend's boy looks like me when the only pussy I've used as a cum bucket is yours, and ironically he's just the right age. I gave you an order. You know what happens when my girls disobey me . . ."

"Please. I'll take him somewhere else. I'll get rid of him a different way. Just let me make it right."

What's she mean get rid of me? I don't understand. I thought she loved me. "I have a better idea," he says. "I think he should see just how he got here."

He shoves her forward, forcing her to bend over the desk. "No!" she screams, fighting to turn around. "Please, just make him leave. Then you can do whatever you want to me."

I back toward the wall, looking around the room for a place to hide. "Come here, little bastard."

"My name is Kross."

He looks at me, a scary smile on his face. "Well, Kross, today we're going to make you a man. We need to raise you up right. I'm going to show you how we deal with women that disobey. Sit in my chair, Son. Only special boys are allowed to sit in that chair."

She tries to stand again but he grabs her hair, pulling her head back, and sticks a knife blade against her throat. He licks her cheek like a cat I saw once. "Keep moving, bitch, and I'll cut up this pretty face. Stand there and take it and I may let you keep him." Why is he doing that to her? Mommy said to never touch knives because they can cut us.

She looks at me, where I'm standing in the corner. She's crying. "It's okay, Kross. Come sit down."

I do as I'm told, climbing up in the big, black chair until my feet are straight out in front of me, my arms on the handles to my sides. "Kross, I used to like your mama; enough to nut in this hot cunt of hers. I used to keep her to myself, instead of sharing her with my customers like the others. She was mine. She had it all. All she had to do was stay mine. I gave her one order and she disobeyed me. She ran off and didn't come back for a few years. She betrayed me. She should really be grateful that I took her broke ass back. And now, after everything I've done for her, I find out that she didn't follow my order at all. In fact, she did the opposite. Do you know what happens when someone doesn't mind their owner?"

"They get a spanking?"

"That's right, except we spank women a different way from boys."

"How?"

"Come here. I'll show you."

"No, Elliot. He's four. Please make him stay there. I'm begging you."

"Shut up, bitch. You brought this on yourself."

I walk around the desk until I'm beside him. I don't want to get a spanking. I cover my eyes with my hands when he pulls her underwear down. I've never seen Mommy without her clothes on before tonight. "Open your eyes."

I do as he says, even though I don't want to. I don't want to make Mommy cry. When I do I see between her legs, but she looks different than me down there. She doesn't have a wee-wee. He pulls his knife toward him, before placing a covering over the sharp part. "If you move I'll slit your throat."

He kicks his boot against the inside of her foot, making her spread her legs. Then he holds the sharp part in his fist, but he doesn't cry like I did when I cut my finger once trying to put jelly on my toast while Mommy was sleeping. He touches her skin with the handle and pushes it against her, making it disappear. She screams, and I cover my eyes again. "Open them, Kross. You need to learn if she's going to bring you around this place. She must be trying to get me closed down with her stupidity. This ain't no place for a kid. There are rules, but she thought you should be here, so you can see what happens when you are."

I lower my hands. His knife keeps going in and out of her body like magic. She's gripping onto the desk, crying loudly. She keeps saying she's sorry, but I don't know what she did. Mommy always tells me what I did wrong if I'm in trouble. He's not telling her what she did wrong before spanking her.

He starts making a funny noise the faster his arm moves, like when I have to stab my plastic shovel hard into the sand to dig the hole. Mommy screams. I cover my ears, but I can still hear the bad words. "I'm going to destroy this cunt, bitch. When I get done with you it won't be possible to carry a bastard kid." Her cries get louder.

He drops his knife to the ground and pushes his pants down to his thighs like he's going to tee-tee. He has my parts, but something *is wrong with it. It's hard. I think it's broken. I pull my hands down, about to ask him why mine doesn't look like that, when he pushes against her, making it disappear like he did his knife. He's spanking her with his body. He's using his wee like Mommy's belt. That's too many times. Mommy said three licks are enough to learn.*

I jump when a loud scream hurts my ears. He's hurting her. He's smiling. He likes hurting her. Mommy cries when she has to hurt me. Red. What's all that red? I run around the desk and hide underneath it, pulling my knees to my chest. I clench my eyes closed, pressing my hands down on my ears and squeezing them. "My wee is bad. I'll never hurt a girl with my wee. I'll never use it." I repeat it three times. "I promise, Mama."

My jaw locks as I pull into the clearing surrounded by large pines. When I finally experienced the rest of that memory for the first time I hurled. I've killed more than a hundred times, many different ways. I've done some pretty sick shit in my life, witnessed even worse by the people I worked for, and none of it has ever made me physically sick. No point of view is worse than seeing something that dark through the mind of a child. It all finally made sense for me. My hatred for sex. My fear of it. My lack of interest in it . . .

I finally realized there wasn't something wrong with me. I just didn't want to become the only person I ever associated with the act. I never realized there were two sides to it, the other being pleasure, until that fucking bitch forced it on me; only making me hate it even more because something I didn't want or consent to felt good. With every unwanted ejaculation I forced myself to control my dick, until finally I could turn off a hard-on with a matter of thoughts. By then, though, I had bulked up in size and my attitude scared her. She stuck with physical abuse and verbal threats by that point, until I was finally old enough to leave and used my dick for the first time as a weapon, a form of revenge, and I made it so that she couldn't ever do what she did to me to anyone else.

I smile, remembering the first kill that made me proud. You should never tell the person you're raping what your deadly allergies are, because one tainted condom is the perfect murder weapon. The body rids of the trace and food allergy deaths are common.

The window between him and I lowers. He has the whisky glass in his hand, almost empty. "Where the fuck are we? This isn't my house."

I breathe in deep, producing a calming effect against the voice that sends my rage into overdrive. "Plans have changed."

I exit the car, quickly making my way to the back, opening his door. He places the glass into the cup holder. "Who are you? You're not my driver."

I lean into the doorframe, further into the light. "Most in your case would call it a son, but I'm going to stick with sperm donor."

I remove the hat, tossing it at him. His eyes widen as he takes in my face, then my tattoos. "You?"

"Again," I taunt, "My name is Kross."

"What are you doing here? You want money or something?"

"I thought you'd be a little happy to see me after all these years, Dad."

He reaches in his suit jacket; my guess going for a gun. "Don't waste your time. By the time you get the barrel to my forehead that Rohypnol that was in your whiskey will be in full effect."

He removes his hand. "What do you want from me? You aren't getting a dime."

I grab his jacket, pulling him toward me. The slight deadening of his body weight proves the drugs are working. I prefer modern methods. It makes my job a hell of a lot easier and less of a mess. I don't prefer leaving my DNA around by having to use my fists on a regular basis. "I guess it's a good thing that I'm a self-made millionaire then, because I only want you."

He tries to push back, shoving the soles of his shiny, black shoes into my abdomen, gaining a few feet as he fumbles around with the door handle, opening the opposite door. I roll my eyes, slamming my door shut before rounding the car just in time for him to fall out. I pull my knife from my leg holster, before squatting to his level, tapping the blade to my lips. He looks at me. His eyes are dilating. He's calming. With every passing minute he's becoming my puppet. "What do you want with me? I let you live."

"That you did. Pity. You should have killed me when you had the chance. I lived in Hell for years because of what you did to her, and now I'm here for you."

"If you had knocked up a stripping whore you'd understand. You don't make girls like her the mother of your child. You didn't live in Hell because of me, but because of her. We didn't plan a kid. She got pregnant behind my back. She should have ended you when I told her to."

I grab his neck, gripping tight. "Oh, I think it's much too late to dwell on should haves. A lot of dead people would probably even agree with you. You're a fucking dumbass. We choose the mother of our children based on the pussy we decide to nut in. The irony in you wanting me gone—I turned out just like you, only better. While you were learning how to overpower women by raping them, manipulating them, controlling them and killing them—a weaker being—I learned how to take out the fucking best. It gives me a high. The harder the kill the better it feels."

"If you're just like me, then join me," he says, his words starting to slur together.

"Not a chance in Hell. I want your soul."

"Why? What is it worth to you?"

"Because I'm fucked up because of you," I scream. "I hated any thought of sex because I watched you mutilate her pussy. My virginity was forced from me because I was a file in the system. I was locked in solitude. Kept from people to protect secrets. I was used and abused. For years I thought my biological mother abandoned me because I couldn't remember anything from that night and before." I hit my head against the flat end of the blade in my hand. "I like to kill. It gives me purpose. I like to deal. It gives me control. I like to tattoo. It relaxes me when the nightmares try to drive me insane. You would have probably had years left, but unfortunately for you, my girl loves me through every fucked up layer, enough to put me out of my goddamned misery. I never asked questions about my past. She did. One file was like a key to everything I had forgotten." I squeeze his neck tighter. "You're going to get a scar just like mine."

I lean in, placing the tip of the blade to his forehead, slicing it in a long downward stroke, my heart pounding at the sight of blood. I raise it again, slashing it in a short, horizontal line, forming a cross. His body is so sedated he doesn't even scream. He's likely not even processing what I'm saying anymore, but I don't care. I need to get the words out. His lids are lazy, but he manages to look at me. "No woman is worth this," he says, barely audible. "Your own blood. I spared you . . . because you're blood. You were even named after me."

I tap the bloody blade against his cross tattoo. "That's where you're wrong. They're all worth something to someone. Her life was worth it to me. My girl's life is fucking priceless. I was going to make this short and painless, but unfortunately for you, the pussy I knocked up is carrying my daughter. I will go on a killing spree before she ends up like one of your girls. She will never see me do the things you did to my mother to hers. I will find it somewhere inside of me to be her father, but this neck piece haunts my dreams. The only way to silence them is to silence you. I'm burying you without it."

I grab his head and shove him to the ground, before straddling his shoulder to hold him still. And then, slowly and meticulously, I do one thing I've never done—ruin another artist's work, outlining it one slice at a time.

CHAPTER SIXTEEN
Kray

I walk through the too tall grass reciting the number in my head as I scan each ID marker attached to the small block of cement it's labeling. I've been walking this public cemetery the state used to use for unclaimed bodies for a while, my feet starting to drag from my boots getting heavier.

I continue forward. It took a lot of fucking hounding to get this information from the social services office. I heard the same shit over and over —'the unclaimed and less fortunate deceased are cremated or donated to science. The state no longer has the funds to provide burials'.

If I heard it once, I heard it ten damn times. And all ten times I told her to check the fucking system because it was twenty-six years ago. I knew before she rechecked the computer that they buried her. Special circumstances and all—her growing up in the system and me being left behind and orphaned—a state official privately paid for a basic burial; a plot and marker.

I stop when the number in front of me matches the one in my head. I stare at it. The small square of cement is blank, not even marking her name. The surrounding grass hasn't seen a weed-eater in way too long. It's as if the existence of her was erased when they laid her in the ground. I may not fear death or pity those I force down that road, but victims like her deserve to be remembered by someone, to be grieved over. Rachel James should be carved into that stone. Not some meaningless number.

I lay the small bouquet of flowers down on the grass that I picked up at the first grocery store I passed. Not the best quality. Didn't cost me but ten bucks, but it felt wrong to show up without them after all this time. I've never been to a cemetery before, but anyone that has a brain knows you bring flowers to those that meant something.

I stand tall, towering over the tiny plot no bigger than a body size, trying to sort through the overload of thoughts racing in my head. I don't know what the fuck to say. I'm not one to talk to myself or believe someone can hear me who's been dead for close to three decades. But I vowed I would come here before I go home—for closure. I meant what I said before I ended him. I have to dig deep to find a man that can make Delta happy, that can be a decent father, even though it's the only thing that truly terrifies me, because somehow I know that I'm going to fuck this up. I have too much bad blood running through my veins.

"I know you can't hear me. Fuck, maybe you can. What do I know anymore? Never walked in the afterlife. I needed you to know that it's done. He paid in your name. Where I failed before I succeeded this time. It started because of me and it ended with me." I grab the flat bill of my hat and twist it toward the side, looking around. For miles it's empty of anyone with life.

"I didn't remember you for a long time, but I remember you now; parts of you. I remember Waffle House breakfasts after you got off. I remember super hero capes made from towels. I remember house sitting for the rich for access to a pool and nicer things for a few days. At least that's what you said we were doing. Now that I'm grown I'm not sure if that was legit or if we were trespassing and that was your cover-up." A single, dry laugh slips. "Maybe I'm more like you than I thought. The most important thing I do remember is there were never any men around. When you were there you were there, mentally and physically. It was just us. You were a good mom with what you had. I know you did the best you could. I don't blame you—for leaving or coming back, for what happened to me. I know you loved me, and even though a lot of shit has changed, that little boy loved you too. So just know, I did it for you, and after all these years I hope you can finally rest in peace. Walk in the light a little brighter knowing there's no one else he can torment."

I place my hands in the pockets of my jeans and take a step back. "Probably won't be back, but maybe I will. I got a girl to look after. Come this summer I'll have two. Girls scare the hell out of me. I fear something will happen to her. I'm worried too much of him is in my blood and one day I'll snap. I told her to end it too. I deserved it when she left me. You would have thought so too. I was a fucking coward. When I looked him in the eyes I couldn't even be mad he wanted me gone. I wanted her gone too. I wanted my girl all to myself. I didn't want the responsibility of a kid. But here I am, about to raise one."

I roll my neck from side to side. "If you're listening, I need you to do me a favor. Tell me when I'm fucking up, when I'm acting like him. When his DNA is overpowering yours. Burn my soul if you have too, but don't let me hurt them. Promise me."

A crow swoops down from the tree branch above, landing on the small cement block, staring at me with its beady eyes, its black coat shining in the sunlight, before it caws twice and flies off.

I smile.

An animal that won't hurt you, but so many fear what its presence represents—something is about to change, a death omen, a spiritual blessing, or confirmation that a powerful human has crossed into the afterlife . . .

I turn and walk away. I'd be worried if it was anything else. Forever a player in the dark. A ruler of the night. The way I see it—that powerful son of a bitch is forever gone. A kingdom overcome.

CHAPTER SEVENTEEN

Detta

I shut off the engine to my car and sit for a moment, my feet hurting, watching the sunset out of my windshield. Layers of pink and orange and navy make up the sky. It was a bad idea to get the massage and pedicure before shopping. I had forgotten exactly how shopping with Lux is. It's not a hobby of leisure at all. It's a damn marathon race. If I had been smart I would have done it last, but my thought was that shopping doesn't have a schedule or waiting list when the other activities I needed to try first before the wait was too long.

I had never been to a full day spa before. I can still feel his fingers kneading deep into my muscles and the hot stones running down my spine. They even had a cutout for pregnant bellies. Badass business tactic. Appeal to the human bodies being used as a host, its energy supply being depleted by something that resembles a tiny alien. I've discovered women in this state would probably pay in organs to get some relief from sciatic nerve mishaps and extra weight bearing down on the small body parts known as my feet. That kind of luxury was created for the privileged; something I've never been before. I had no idea an Amex of certain colors held so much power. Whip out that piece of plastic and you become royalty. I tried not to look at the ungodly amount charged to that card that Kross was okay with paying as I signed the digital box.

I reach over and grab my purse from the passenger seat. A text message dings through the car speakers connected to my phone's Bluetooth—the music still playing since I haven't opened the driver's side door—instantly making me smile.

Kross: Headed your way. See you in a few hours.

Before I can answer another text comes through.

Kross: Put on something sexy. Leave the bottoms off.

I shiver. A contradiction to the fire burning in my cheeks.

Me: I'm not sure anything can be sexy with a half deflated basketball underneath it. No panties—consider it done. I'll try to wait up for you.

He quickly responds. My guess is he isn't even on the plane yet.

Kross: That's why I'm the one with the dick and not you.

I bite my bottom lip, already halfway to a grin.

Me: One that I have missed very much, might I add.

Kross: You'll take that back when it's done with you. I'm boarding. I better come home to new shit.

Me: Okay. Be safe. I love you.

Kross: I love you too. Both of you.

A tear falls down my cheek. He acknowledged her. I quickly swipe it away. We're going to be okay. I've been worried how he would return with the extended separation. I wasn't expecting his absence to be so long. Thoughts ran wild that he would change his mind once he was back to being alone, doing things he needed to do without anything slowing him down, but I was wrong to have those thoughts. We may have a crazy life, one that most wouldn't understand, but things get a little better every day.

I hate thinking of what he did last night and to Chuck, deserved or not. It's especially difficult to process that someone you spent a length of your life with now being dead, regardless of whether they were good for you or bad. It took me a while to come to peace with the arms dealing. Murder—I'm still working on. Knowing that's only a crack in the surface to what all he really does is hard to fathom. Sometimes it's even painful to stomach. I don't think any human being with a conscience would be okay with their significant other taking a life so freely, but love isn't judgmental, and it certainly isn't controllable, so I somehow find a way to deal. On a good day I feel like the devil's lover. Kross is truly a scary man, and I don't know the half of it.

I open the door and press the release to the trunk before getting out. I open the back as soon as I get to it, inspecting the damage I did with the help of Lux. "You're going to come home to new shit all right. Lots of pink." At least I was smart enough to put the smaller bags inside of the bigger bags. I start sliding bag handles up each arm until I'm loaded down, my keys in hand. I pull the trunk down, maneuvering myself to get it latched before heading toward the house. I probably should have pulled into the garage, but the view was pretty spectacular. I'll do it tomorrow.

I shove the key into the lock and turn it. At least the front door has a handle with a press down latch versus a knob. I don't want to have to put stuff down and start the whole process over again. I press on the latch with the outside of my fist and shove the door open with my hip, before walking inside. I drop the bags at my feet and turn back around to shut the door and search for the light switch. It takes me a while to find this one in the dark because we never use this door.

I scream when a set of hands touch my hips. "Kross?"

I'm forced against a body that I immediately know isn't his based on the extra body fat alone, panic rising inside of me. I try to push myself forward, toward the wall with the switch to eliminate this darkness, but I'm gripped harder against him, my arms rendered useless by his, the pointed end of a nose running down the length of my neck. His hand rubs across my swollen belly, a wave of nausea building in my stomach. "Please, don't hurt me. I'll give you whatever you want. Just name it."

He laughs in my ear. "There's nothing you have that I want, sweetness," he says, accent thick and non-American. He runs his hand down my pelvis, before squeezing hard between my legs. "Or maybe there is."

Reflexively I press my legs together, my heart pounding and my pulse raging in my ears. "Don't. Please. Let me go."

He laughs manically, removing his hand. "No can do. You see, Güzel, I'm a very powerful man. A man that gets what he wants, and I pay for my wants well. No one tells me no. No man has ever turned down my offer. For now, what I want is you. Let's see just how much you're worth to that gun-slinging boyfriend of yours. When he gives me what I want, I'll give him you."

My entire body goes on high alert. My adrenaline spikes and surges through every vessel in my body. All I can think about is protecting her. She's not ready. I need to stay alive . . . for her. I begin to fight against him, trying to get to my cell phone. "Help! Somebody!"

He shoves me against the door, making it impossible to kick or move. His body weight is overpowering mine. His lips touch against my ear. I jerk away, crying into the empty house. Kross. The only one that can help me is on a plane. By the time he gets here I could be in another country somewhere. "He shouldn't have brought you to his business meeting. I knew there was something special about you when he sent you to the bar. I can certainly see the appeal. I've been watching you, and when I saw this . . ." He touches my belly again, making me feel dirty. "It confirmed you were even more valuable than I thought." He licks up my neck. I scream out in disgust, putting every ounce of energy I can muster into fighting him off.

I run when I catch him off guard, gaining just enough space to get free, but he grabs my hair in his fist, jerking me backward until I stumbling. He catches me before I hit the ground, pulling me against him again. "Don't do that, Güzel. You wouldn't want to hurt her, would you?" I freeze. "I need everyone unharmed to ensure this goes as planned."

"He will kill you," I breathe out, the stress taking over.

"Not if he wants you alive," he seethes, and then a handkerchief is forced over my mouth, a strange smell dousing it. I scream again, kicking and jerking, but within seconds everything is fading into nothingness, Kross' face the last thing I see.

Kross

I grab the energy drink out of the cup holder and finish it off. It's definitely not as effective as blow, but it gets the job done. I'm running on maybe an hour of sleep out of the last forty-eight, but I don't plan on catching up tonight. Sleep is not in the plans for what I'm going to do to her when I get there, which will be in about ten minutes.

I turn on the last road before it hits nothing but wide-open countryside. I like my privacy and I paid well for it. The longer drive into the city than most people prefer proves it.

I turn into the drive, my headlights reflecting off the taillights of her car as I approach the house. It's out of place; pulled up close to the closed garage off to the side, but not in it. Expensive cars shouldn't be left out in the weather, making them easier to steal in the dead of night. Fucking women. I pull up beside her and stop, shifting my truck into park, the garage door already opening as I get out. I take the spare key and shove myself inside, moving her car into the garage. At least she keeps it clean.

On the walk back to my truck the floodlight comes on as I pass the sensor. I grab the open door and go to get in my truck when something on the porch draws my attention. What the hell? The front door is cracked, but the lights are off. That's not like her.

I kill the engine and get back out of my truck, before walking to the porch, turning on the flashlight to my cell phone along the way. I hold it up to the door, inspecting it to see that everything is how it should be. Nothing looks forced. I push it open, quickly turning on the light to shopping bags scattered all around the entry. Her purse is also there, lying on the floor with its contents spilling out, including her phone. Something isn't right. She's not a slob. I've lived with her long enough to know she at least moves shit away from the door. "Delta," I shout. Fuck, maybe she was tired and just forgot to close the damn door.

I get no response. "Delta," I holler louder. Still nothing. I slam the door and drop my keys on the entry table, before making my way through the dark house toward our bedroom. The second the light comes on I know she's not here. The bed is made as if no one has been in it all day, but a large yellow envelope is sitting on top— one that looks familiar.

I stare at it, the possibilities mapping out in my mind. Nothing fucking happened in my house, on my property. I have cameras everywhere. There's no way. My phone would have alerted me . . . unless. The plane. No. That's too fucking convenient. I back out of the room, before storming every inch of the house, each room coming up short. The house is cleaner than when I left it.

I end up back inside my bedroom, arms crossed over my chest, staring at that motherfucking envelope. Minutes pass as every plausible explanation for her absence plays out. My foot inches forward, and before the clock changes to the next minute I'm picking it up, inspecting it. Either the same envelope I left for pickup all those weeks ago has sprouted limbs and walked here or someone put it there. I open it, finding the same burner cell phone inside.

I pull it out, the instructions labeled on the front with a sticky note. As ordered, I place the call and hold the phone to my ear, the all-consuming rage running rampant in my body to the point that I can't think. It rings twice before the line picks up. "I've been expecting your call, Mr. Brannon."

"Where is she?"

"I'm afraid that's not how this works. This will go my way. I tried your way."

"I'm not stealing a classified military grade missile for you. I gave you contacts for other dealers that'd jump on the offer."

"Those other dealers don't have the reputation that you do. I've been led to believe that you can get anything. I was informed you were the man that doesn't put anything in front of a job."

"That was before. No one forces a job on me. I don't take orders. Now tell me, where the fuck is she?"

A ripping sound comes through the phone, followed by her scream. My fist locks. A level of wrath I've never experienced takes over. "Please don't touch me. Not again," she cries, and every ounce of blood in my body runs cold.

"Tell him, Güzel. Tell him to save you."

She cries louder. "Kross, do whatever it takes. Save *her*."

"Bring me the missile and I'll deliver the girl . . . or should I say both."

"You remove so much as a hair on her fucking head and I'll send your head to your family."

"The instructions are in the envelope. Don't disappoint me or I'll send her to the Lions' den. She is appetizing. My boys will have fun devouring her."

He disconnects the call.

I pull my phone out of my pocket as I rush through the house toward the basement. A few rings and he picks up, his voice groggy. "Yeah."

"You remember that favor you owe me?"

He's silent for a few seconds.

"Since your girl is in bed with you I'm going to say that you do. It's time to collect."

"What is it? Do you know what time it is? Some of us go to sleep at normal times when we aren't on a job . . ."

"They took her. You got your girl. I'm going to get mine. I could probably take them myself, but I'd be wasting unnecessary time."

"Fucking slow down. Who took her?"

"Who is that? Took who?" Lux says in the background.

"Kross," he barks into the phone. "Time wasted is distance they gain. Who?"

"I turned down a job. A big one. I'm not usually one to be picky over the details. Millions are millions, but the accent, the dress, the type of missile he's wanting—it didn't feel right. Too much terrorist shit is going on already. Paranoia is high. People are scared. Government is overly cautious. Crime is my game, dealing is my way, but I'm not into treason. Then the pregnancy happened. I said no. Apparently he's pissed off and figured out my weak spot. I made an amateur mistake."

"Shit. How many are we looking at?"

"I don't know." I run down the stairs until I'm in the basement. I uncover and punch in the key code to my underground vault; the one Delta hasn't even been in. It's for an emergency—end of time type shit. It's loaded down. Every square inch is covered with weapons and ammo, from small caliber to big. It's enough to make it through a fucking zombie apocalypse.

Lux is whisper-shouting things in the background, panic in her voice. I stare straight ahead; mesmerized at its glory. "Why do you seem so calm? Your girl has been abducted. I'd be losing my shit."

I grab a silencer. "I was bred to kill. Shown violence from an early age. Raised up to hate. Revenge is fun. Panic ensues mistakes. My rage is released with body count. He crossed the wrong bastard. I'm going for his head; won't stop until he's dead." I glance at the sniper rifles only granted to the best. "You think Chevy wants a break from your boring domesticated lifestyle? I need a sniper."

"I'll bring him. We'll meet you there. I need an hour."

"This is war, Kaston. Leave your morals at home. Bring the fucking rain."

CHAPTER EIGHTEEN

Kaston

A knock at the door signifies Chevy has arrived. I should have known it wouldn't take him long to get here. I'm starting to wonder if he ever goes home. He's the first one at the office and the last to leave, aside from me. He's always out in the field. At night he's at his club. He never speaks of home, if he speaks at all. He prefers to watch more than anything. I never see him with girls. He seems almost tortured at the mention of one.

"Lux, I'm about to head out," I shout as I pick up the small bag full of gear, opening the door. Chevy is standing on the other side, dressed in all dark clothing, his face even dusted in black. "You ready to do this? We've had no prep time. This isn't like our normal jobs."

"As ready as I am to hold a gun for a purpose. I've been to war. I know how to fight."

I nod, taking a step out the door. "Wait." Lux comes walking through the house fully dressed in tight, black clothes, riding boots on her feet, and her hair braided down the back. If I didn't have something important to do I'd go back in there and strip her down.

"Where are you going?"

"With you."

"No you're not. You're going to stay here."

Her hands go to her hips, challenging me. "I wasn't aware I had to follow orders from you."

I glance at Chevy, before turning away from the knowing gleam in his eyes. I wish the fucker would find someone already so I can wipe that smirk off his face. "Lux, this isn't like in the movies. You don't just swoop in and grab the girl from the villains. These people are dangerous. They're crime lords. This isn't the kind of people I normally go after. Kross and I have an understanding. We do some of the same crimes, but we come from two different underworlds. I won't be able to concentrate if I'm having to watch you."

"Kaston, I wasn't asking. She's my best friend. She's been more of a sister to me than what I'd consider blood. She's carrying my niece—for all intents and purposes. There isn't a dark time I was in that she wasn't there for me. I'm going. End of discussion. Give me a gun and I'll follow your lead. I killed someone once. When it comes to family, I'd do it again in a heartbeat."

"I don't want my future wife there. Look at you. You're bang bait. No. You need to let us handle this."

"Like he handled keeping her safe? You promised me I wouldn't have to worry about her when I told you how she felt about him. You said he'd protect her, just like you'd protect me. She's not like us. Don't let her sass fool you. Delta is . . . fragile."

"And I meant it. He's the most capable person I know. And honestly, probably more so than me. He doesn't have his emotions standing in his way." I take a deep breath. "I need you to stay."

"No."

"Kaston, we need to go," Chevy interrupts.

"Fuck," I whisper. "This is going to piss him off."

"I'm not scared of Kross."

I reach in the table drawer by the door and extend the handgun toward her. "You should be," I say. "Don't get cocky just because I pulled you out of his way once. He's a lot scarier than he looks. If he were faced with the devil himself I'd bet on Kross."

She takes the gun. "Holster it. I swear to God, if you don't follow my orders you'll regret it when I get you home. I may love you, but I'm still your man. At the end of the day there can only be one alpha, and it will always be me. Let's ride."

And just like I'd expect, she storms out the door, brushing past Chevy toward the furthest end of the garage. I hope this doesn't get messy. My dad hasn't spent my entire life teaching me how to be invisible for me to fuck up now.

Lux

I stare out the back window of Chevy's SUV as we pull into the driveway, coming to a stop in front of the garage. My mind is racing a million miles a minute, wondering what in the hell they're doing to her. The thoughts bring back the memories, and the memories bring back the emotions of being someone's puppet. And once again an innocent baby is stuck in the middle.

Men don't understand what it's like to be a female. We're always deemed the weaker party. Expected to keep quiet and be obedient.

When someone is used for blackmail it's always us. Our bodies are the ones that get put on display for sick pleasure, and abused as if it's only an object. I've spent years training myself to be anything but those things after everything I went through.

My obedience is what got me pregnant. My silence, in my eyes, is what put my daughter in the ground. My body was used to pay a debt, over and over. I will never be silent again. I will never obey when there is something at stake. She is my best friend. I will not play it safe when she's in trouble. I will not sit at home as if it's a typical Friday night while she's out there somewhere, probably experiencing something horrible at the hands of a man. I will lay everything down to try to bring her home, even if it's my own life. That's what you do for family. You sacrifice. You protect them. You seek vengeance on those that harm them. That baby means the most of all. She has no way to protect herself. She relies on us. I will not bury another baby.

Kross walks out the front door carrying one large bag strapped to his back and one in each hand. They must be heavy the way his tattooed neck muscles are strained underneath the light of a full moon. He's wearing dark jeans and a black, long sleeve thermal, a knife strapped to his upper arm and weapons attached to his belt. Jeez, I wonder what he has hidden if all of that is in plain sight.

I can't read his expression like I can most people. It's completely void. I'm not sure I've ever seen the man crack a smile except for that brief encounter all those months ago when we walked in his tattoo shop. I can't tell if he's angry, if he's worried, or if he's sad. That's what worries me most of all. I want to know the loss of her is enough to destroy him. That's the kind of love she deserves more than anything.

He walks to the rear of the SUV and opens the back, putting

the bags inside. I turn around when the overhead light comes on. His eyes fall on me almost immediately, before he looks at Kaston in the front seat, disregarding me completely. "What's she doing here? Have you lost your goddamned mind?"

"Just leave it alone. It's her best friend. The argument is dead in the water."

"Yeah, well, she's your problem if shit goes south. You're crossing a very distinct line. You're exposing someone important to you to people that look for something to use against you. My focus is on one. The rest of you know how to take care of yourself. She's going to be in the way."

"Fuck you, Kross. In case you missed it, I'm right here. You have something to say about me you can say it to me, not to my fiancé. I'm a big girl. I made the decision to come on my own. You got her into this shit and we're helping you. Stop being a fucking asshole. She's no less important to me than she is you. If anything she's more. Accept that you have to share her and move on."

"Watch your back," he says, and with no other response he shuts the back and walks around to the other side.

Kaston turns around, cutting his eyes at me for back talking, pissed as all hell. "What?" I whisper-shout. "I don't like being talked over." I shut up when Kross opens the back door, getting into the vehicle. Before the overhead light fades out from him shutting the door I notice something pink gripped in his fist, laid over his thigh. It's so dainty and obvious against the dark ink covering the back of his hand; so small compared to his large size. I think back to all the stuff we bought for Emery yesterday. It was a lot of clothes because she was finally buying some things so we went a little crazy since she had nothing prior. I finally remember the small, long sleeve newborn onesie that said 'Daddy's girl'.

It was part of a five-piece set, so if he's holding that then he's gone through the bags. A man that does not care doesn't go through shopping bags. A man that does not care doesn't risk everything to go after her. He cuts his losses. I welcome the relief amongst the worry. Maybe I was a bitch. So, even though I hate apologies . . . "I'm sorry, Kross. I didn't mean—"

"When she's back . . ." he interrupts, looking out of his window. "When they're back, I need you to help her with the baby's room. I'll give you the fucking money since she's stubborn. Get whatever she needs. All I saw in there were clothes. I may not know shit about babies, but I'm smart enough to know they need more than that."

I smile in the dark, realizing that he didn't say 'if' but 'when' and that choice of wording makes all the difference in the world. Chevy backs up and pulls out into the drive. "Okay, Kross. I can do that."

Shopping . . . I can definitely do that.

CHAPTER NINETEEN

Kross

We all pile out as soon as Chevy backs into an alley. It's a few blocks from the old factory about an hour outside of town that hasn't been in operation in at least fifteen years. The several surrounding buildings make up an old rural town that eventually became nothing as most businesses migrated to more urban parts of the state. All it is now is a ghost town. It's fallen off the grid of law enforcement. Places like this are mostly used as shelters for drug addicts. Too bad I didn't find it first.

I open the back and grab one of the two bags, handing it to Chevy. "Everything you need is in the bag. Take the east side. There is an old fire-training tower with easy access to the top. Kill anything that moves. Lux can be your spotter. It'll keep her safe."

"I'm not doing that. I can go with Kaston," she says, running her mouth; a thing I've realized women do best, especially her. Irrational thinking. Wanting to have the last say. Not concerned about the safety of anyone else.

I glance at her, pulling out the other bag. "It's the logical way, but it's your life. I am not going to argue."

I extend the other bag toward Kaston. "You're going, Lux," he says. "End of discussion. Following orders was the deal for you to come."

"Kaston—"

He combs his hands through her hair, tilting her head back, and then he kisses her. Not really the time or place. "Stop fucking arguing. That's the most important job of any of us. You're his eyes. You're my protection. Watch my back, baby. Be my eyes."

"Okay, fine." I raise my brow at the soft tone of his voice. Apparently my methods are more cut and dry. Delta listens just fine without all that serenading shit.

She runs to catch up to Chevy's retreating form about twenty feet away. Kaston finally grabs the bag from me. "Not a fucking word. Women are a lot like weapons. They all operate about the same, but each one handles a little differently. With practice you find the best fit, the right alignment. She backfires if you force her."

"Which is why she's with you and not me. I don't conform to the weapon; the weapon conforms to me. Take the north. They aren't expecting us for two days. To them it's a waiting game. We take them by surprise, wipe them out, and get my girl. I'll take the south side. Spare no one. They crossed me. They pay. That's my only way. How you do it is up to you."

I grab the final bag and pull it on my back before closing the door. We both walk down the alley until it's time to split. He goes one way. I go the other. "Kross."

I stop.

"Why is your bag so much smaller?"

I inhale, familiarizing myself with the scent in the air. "For me this is personal. I'm harvesting body parts. I don't need a gun for that."

No, a knife will serve me just fine, and they come in many different shapes and sizes. They're about to find out exactly what earned me my reputation.

Bones and blood—what I hunt.

I stand in the shadows. just off the service road away from the security light, watching the back entrance. Two cars ornament the empty lot. The faded wavy metal of the building is speckled with rust spots. I memorize my surroundings. There is only one light on at the furthest window to the right, second floor—likely a camping lantern or something similar. I close my eyes, laying out the blueprint I dug up online in my head. I'd bet everything I own that's where she is.

One is guarding the door, always. If he walks away another falls into place, but for the last twenty minutes it's been just him and no other activity. Suddenly that crow makes a lot of fucking sense. I read its sign wrong. Their presence always means something. I should have paid attention.

I close my eyes, preparing to kill. I remember the first promise I ever made to myself, before I took a life.

Life is a game.

Evil prevails. Those that spill blood win. Death is a loss.

Respect is to be fought for.

The battle is silencing the mind.

No one can be trusted.

Always look out for self.

Persevere until the job is done.

Souls of the innocent are to be left untouched.

Darkness only takes souls of the wicked.

And the most important part of all . . .

In the rare occurrence that you learn to love, or that someone loves you, protect her at all costs. Slaughter those that stand in the way.

They tried to take her from me. The only girl I've ever wanted. The first to love me for me—bloodstained hands and all. The craving comes alive. Adrenaline feeds my racing heart. Rage flows through my veins. First comes love, and then comes war.

I step out into the light and walk toward him when he turns to light a smoke. I draw my skinning knife from my boot, turning it in my hand as I approach. He looks up when my boot hits a piece of loose gravel. "Hey, aren't you—"

I swing my arm out, gliding the blade of my knife across his trachea, silencing him. I grip his neck, blood pouring down the front, pushing him against the metal building as warm, thick liquid coats the inside of my hand. "Where the fuck is your boss?"

A gargling sound comes from his mouth. He reaches for his gun. I drive my knife into his hand until the tip hits bone. A panicked breath occurs. "Find a way to tell me or I'll cut you ear to ear. He fucked with the wrong dealer."

He cuts his eyes to his left, my right. "Second floor with the light? Blink once for yes, twice for no." He blinks once. "He have my girl?" Another single blink. I retrieve my knife from his hand and shove him to the ground, coming up behind him. The sole of my boot plants at the middle of his back with force, sending him surging forward.

I squat behind him, pulling his shoulder length hair toward me to get the right angle. "Hell hath no fury like a man in love. Should have sat this one out," I say, before slicing my knife from one jugular to the other, blood spurting with every heartbeat until his body lay lifeless on the ground.

I stand and wipe my knife on my jeans, my arms covered in his blood, before turning toward the closed door. One down, the rest to go. I'm coming for you motherfucker, head and all.

Delta

A gunshot rings out in the distance. waking me, and sending my heart into overdrive. I jar the back of my head on the dirty wall from the sudden noise. My arms reflexively pull on the chains attached to the industrial beams running overhead throughout the building, the cuffs around my wrists digging into my skin.

I've been standing here for what seems like days, even though it's likely been hours. My entire body is sore, and I've been forced to pee in the bucket between my legs, my panties and leggings removed from my body by another man the first time I had to go. They've taken turns standing in the room, looking at me, gawking at my nakedness, and making sexual slurs about my body. I feel dirtier than I ever did stripping or with Chuck. I want to go home. I've cried until I feel thirsty and my cheekbone is freshly bruised from the last time I tried to fight against another man's touch.

Another shot rings out and two men run in the room, followed by the man that took me. "Move her," he commands, the other two coming toward me. I try hard to kick, but my legs are so heavy they barely leave the floor. "Take her to the car. He's stupider than I thought. He'll never get past my army."

He cuts in front of them until his body is directly in front of me, his hands instantly groping my ass, squeezing and kneading each cheek. I try to kick him in the balls, but he grips my thigh, placing his fingers against my lips. I gather every ounce of moisture left and spit in his face. "Don't fucking touch me."

His fist connects with my jaw, blood spewing out of my mouth from the hit. He rubs my spit back on my face with his, his teeth bared outside my ear. "Sounds like I get to have some fun with you after all," he seethes. "That's just too bad. I was willing to leave you alone, but I won't be made a joke. I'm going to fuck that pretty little cunt until you bleed."

"No. Please," I beg, trying to push myself against the wall. He grabs my face, swiping his tongue over the place he hit, taunting me. The fear settles deep within my bones. Emery hasn't moved in a while, worrying me. I finally started feeling her move recently. They're subtle, but they're there. And now I depend on that feeling at least a few times a day. I'm fighting not to think about what that could mean.

"Change of plans," he says, the other two coming up behind him. "Take her to my office. I want it to be seen when I take her." He backs away, leaving me to his little sidekicks. One wraps his hands around mine, attempting to remove the cuffs holding me in place. I rock my body with all my might, trying and failing miserably to shove him off.

Glass shatters, and within seconds he falls to the ground in front of me, not moving, blood pooling under his head. The other guy runs toward me, grabbing the key from his still hand, hurriedly replacing him when his eyes stop moving and blood begins running down his nose. I scream when I realize it's from a small hole between his eyes, and the screaming continues when I glance down, both of them laying on the floor, lifeless, their eyes void and open. The man responsible for all of this runs out of the room like a coward, leaving me to die with no chance to run.

A full on panic ensues, as I pull on the chains so hard that the metal against my skin is drawing blood, cries hindering my breathing as fear runs rampant through my body. The room resembles a horror scene. I am trying to pretend I don't know what the soft matter splattered against the wall beside me is. My entire past life flashes before my eyes. My future—the life I didn't get to have—follows. Kross. Emery. I don't want to die. I don't want to lose her. I've felt her. She's too real.

I close my eyes, screaming through the noises, trying to tune out the gory sounds outside of the room that seem to go on forever. I don't even want to attempt to match what sound belongs to what act—grunts, slicing, sounds of wetness, thuds and falls. My face is soaked from my tears. The inside of my thighs are wet from the accident I just had.

Then everything suddenly goes silent. A deafening sound that means something horrible is about to happen. Footsteps. I hear footsteps. They're getting closer. I bow my head, pulling into myself when I feel the presence of someone else a few inches away. "Please don't hurt me."

A hand touches the outside of my thigh, migrating inward. "No! Please. Don't do this!" I try to force my legs together, the bucket stopping me. He doesn't stop his exploration over my entire body. I cry harder, waiting for the moment I've been dreading since I was taken. The moment when my choice is taken from me. My entire body shakes. I fight to go to my happy place. A place that Kross is holding me and we have Emery.

"Delta."

"Kross, I'm so sorry. I love you."

"Delta."

"Just do it already!" I scream, my voice giving out.

Hands grip my face. "Delta, it's me. Recognize my touch."

Sobs rack my body over his voice in my head. It's a cruel trick for your mind to play on you in a state of distress. "I tried to protect her."

Lips touch mine. I clench mine together, preventing entry. He continues to kiss me, until finally, I kiss him back, recognizing who is standing in front of me. He pulls away and the sobbing returns. "You came for me."

"Delta. Open your eyes."

With a single command they open. I blink, over and over, before the panic starts all over again as I take him in. Blood. Blood is everywhere. It's covering his clothes. It's dried on his skin. It's wet from the fresh. It's stained on his hands. I don't know where it's coming from, or who it belongs to. "Are you hurt?"

"No."

"Where are they all?"

"Hell."

"What did you do to . . . him?"

"Kept a promise."

"Where did all that blood come from?"

"You don't want to know."

My chest is heaving. I nod toward the two lying in the floor. "And them?"

"Chevy."

With every breath I relax a little more. "Who else is here?"

"Kaston and Lux."

My eyes well up all over again. "You came for me."

He wipes my tears. "You're my girl. The road to forever may be paved in blood, but I'll always come for you."

"I've missed you so damn much." With every wipe of my tears new ones come.

He kicks the bucket out of the way and kneels in front of me, placing his large hands on my belly. "Delta," he pauses. "Did they . . ."

"No." His forehead falls against my belly with the answer. "Kross, she isn't moving. She hasn't in a while. What if she . . ."

He grabs the bottom of my tunic, pushing it up my body until my swollen belly is uncovered. My bottom half is bare. I have no idea where they took my leggings and panties. I've been cold for so long I can't even tell anymore. I wish I had my hands. I want to wrap them around his neck so bad.

His lips find their way to my skin, just above my belly button, his hands still pressed against the sides. "Emery," he says in a voice so deep against me that could alter the universe. "Daddy is here."

And for the first time in hours, I feel her move. "Thank God," I cry. Emotions flood my mind. Relief consumes my body. Kaston walks in the room, quickly cutting the chain between the cuffs, before grabbing the two bodies and dragging them from the room, never looking at my half naked body or commenting on Kross still pressed against my stomach.

I wrap my hands around his head despite being freaked out over the blood, and even though I want to cover myself, to go home, to shower off this filth and lay in our bed for days with him, I don't, because for the first time in this pregnancy Kross is coming to terms with being a father, and that's worth more than anything else.

EPILOGUE

Delta

"Hey, baby girl, it's Aunt Lux. We've been waiting a long time to meet you." I glance across the room at Emery bundled up in Lux's arms, listening to Lux talk to her. Kaston is sitting beside her, his hand cupped around the back of Emery's head and his other arm stretched out behind Lux on the small sleeper sofa in the hospital room. He's staring at Lux interacting with her, adoration in his eyes.

A knock sounds at the door, a young postpartum nurse not much older than me walking in pushing her computer station toward me. She's a different one than I've had since they moved me into a postpartum room, signifying it's likely a shift change. "How you feeling, Mama?"

I hold out my wrist when she extends the handheld scanner toward me, letting her scan my wristband. "Tired," I admit, feeling every minute of the past thirteen hour labor and thirty minute pushing session that only ended an hour ago.

She types something in her computer. "Are you in pain?"

I raise my brow when she looks back at me, pulling a pen from her scrub pocket. "Is that a trick question? I just pushed a six-pound watermelon out of my vagina; my very normal sized, petite girl vagina. It's screaming at me."

She laughs. "I'm glad you're honest. Between you and me, I want to slap those women that look at me with tears in their eyes and say, 'I'm great.' So, would you like some medication to ease the pain or are you going to be like them and try to be a super hero in the days of modern medicine?"

"Drug me up."

A few clicks on her computer and she hands me a small cup with two pills inside. I take it with the glass of water on the rolling tray beside me, handing the empty cup back to her. "I'll check on you in a little while." She glances at Kaston and Lux still holding Emery, and then back at me as she starts pushing her cart to the door, hinting not so subtly. "Try to get some rest. You have all day tomorrow for visitors."

After fighting with Kross about going in to work this morning when he wanted me to stay home and rest, I waddled my ass in the front door with him on my tail, just in time for my water to break behind the desk as I was booting up the computer. Didn't even have a chance to put my purse down before I was staring down at a puddle of liquid on the floor. I couldn't get the mop out of the closet to clean it up before the 'I told you so started' and lots of cursing followed. My goal was to work through the milder contractions. He had me in the truck and headed to the hospital within five minutes, leaving my embarrassing mess for Cassie to clean up; all to just lay there for hours on end, feeling every ounce of pain until I couldn't take it anymore. An epidural is an amazing thing. I went from crying and breathing and whining and squeezing to floating on a magical pain free cloud within minutes, my entire lower body useless.

I swear that man has some kind of connection with the universe, a ruler of all things supernatural, because I had not had one single contraction the entire pregnancy; not even Braxton Hicks. And at thirty-nine weeks and two days, she had more time to bake before her arrival date. The two of them were plotting against me just for spite, because the 'apprentice' discounted tattoos have been doing so well over the past several months. I've gotten more hours in with the gun than I ever imagined—even following Kross' strict hour-long break requirement between sessions to get up and walk around, due to the pregnancy and all.

Now, I'll be out for at least six weeks, according to my doctor. I wish I had been told that at any appointment except for the one Kross was present for. There is no chance of me returning early with him having that knowledge. Every time I think about it I want to roll my eyes and smile at the same time.

When we got back home after my 'abduction from Hell', I took a few weeks off to gather my bearings. I stood in the shower that night for two hours, crying and shaking under the hot and cold water as the shock wore off, Kross with me the entire time. Truth is I was scared. I could have lost so much more than I did; like my life, my baby, and my own control over my body. I needed to get my mind right after that, and some nights, the nightmares are still real. Those hours of darkness were a turning point for me. I promised never again to take advantage of my life, of the people important to me. Instead, I want to value it. I'm done living like I have too much time. Now, I live as if I may not get another day, and it's the best damn thing I've ever done.

We vowed not to talk about it once it was over—all of us. It was my request. It's best that way. The man I love can stomach a lot that I can't. I saw things that night I never thought I would. Things I never want to see again. Kross refused to tell me what he did to that man. I had to know, for me, so I asked. I could see darkness in Kross' eyes that night that terrified me. I knew whatever he did was bad. Deep down I know he deserved whatever he got, but despite everything I went through with my mom growing up, I somehow was granted a tender, caring heart, and death is something that can't be reversed. I think Kross knows it too, because to this date he has yet to confess. But the part he doesn't know is that when he carried me out, my arms wrapped around his neck, I got a glimpse of a corpse Kaston was dealing with missing a very important body part. It made the headless horseman story come to life, and something like that, unfortunately, I'll never forget, as much as I wish I could.

Kross refuses to leave me since that night. He won't admit it, but I think he's adopted guilt over what happened; that maybe some of it was his fault, even though that's absurd. I could have said no to anything he made me a part of, but I didn't. He stayed with me when I wouldn't work, and he's not taken any jobs outside of the shop since; at least not directly. I'm pretty sure Kross has an entire black-market organization out there that he can work from behind the scenes; all in which I'm not completely familiar with yet.

What I do know is that he's spent more time with his designs and the company that Kaston is investing in. His new stuff that's been stored in a warehouse not far away will go in the new shop across town. If it goes well, he will revamp all of his existing shops, eliminating a lot of his third party vendors. I know there are things that are part of him I can't change, and honestly, even after everything, I don't want to. If you love someone you accept them the way they are. It's one major breakthrough my mom and I have had throughout the past months of my pregnancy. She's learning to love me outwardly for who I am, tattoos, piercings and all, and she'll be waiting at our house with my stepdad to meet Emery once we get home. Because of the chemotherapy her immune system is compromised and a hospital is the last place she needs to be.

As for mine and Kross' life—I don't have to be okay with crime to accept it. There is always a cause and effect. Kross' lifestyle is the effect of his childhood. I love him, I understand him, and I accept him . . . fully. The way he lives doesn't affect his love for me, which gets more obvious every day.

We decided on the night that we stood in Emery's completed pink and black room, decorated in feminine skulls and crossbones and packed with everything she needs and then some that I would stay behind when he had a job or a meeting from now on. I'll be the one to raise Emery behind the scenes when there are things he has to do. After he realized in a back and forth discussion I will not be babysat on nights he has to leave me, he doubled up on security in all forms at home. He's been teaching me how to shoot with target practice to protect myself if I ever need it, so it's unnecessary, but I deal with it if it makes him feel better.

I lay my head back against the elevated hospital bed and look at Kross, who's standing in the corner not far from Lux with his hands in his pockets, staring at Emery. His expression is void, so I know he's working feelings or thoughts out in his head, and I've let him with no disruption. He's been there the entire time we've been in this room, doing the same thing. The only difference in now and during labor and delivery was he did stand beside me at the head of the bed then. He looks more like a gargoyle than a person. Kaston gave up trying to talk to him a while ago. A few questions unanswered and a knowing look and he hasn't acknowledged Kross since. Those two have a relationship I'll probably never understand, so I don't even try.

But he's yet to hold his daughter.

"Lux, can you guys give us a few minutes alone? I'm tired and I need to talk to Kross about something."

She stands slowly and walks toward me. Kross' eyes never leave Emery as she crosses the room. She smirks when she gets close enough that she's away from the boys. "Someone is protective," she whispers, placing Emery in my arms. Emery makes a noise as she yawns and resettles. I notice Kross tense out of the corner of my eye. Lux places her hands on my face, kissing my forehead. "You did good, Mama. We're going to get out of here. I'm starving and hospital food is not for me. Call me if you need anything. I'm just a drive away."

"Okay. Love you. Tell the nurse no visitors, will ya?"

"Sure thing." She winks, before turning and gathering her things. Kross moves to the sleeper as Kaston and Lux walk to the door, leaning forward and placing his forearms to his thighs, his hands rubbing up and down his face.

The door finally shuts. "Kross."

He looks at me. "Come hold her."

He stares at her for a moment, and then looks at me. "She's better with you. I'm fine."

I'm going to have to go about this differently. "Come here. You're making me feel like I have a contagious disease."

He stands and walks over to me. "I figured you needed space after . . . all that."

"What I need is for you to sit in that chair next to me."

Surprisingly, he doesn't argue. He does as I asked. I slowly maneuver myself to the edge of the bed with her in my arms. He stands in a hurry. "What do you need? I'll get it."

"Sit, Kross," I say, harsher. "I had a baby. I'm not helpless."

He blows out but does as I ask. When I get my feet on the ground I slowly stand and step toward him, forcing her in his arms. Every muscle tenses to cradle her when I let go. "I'm going to shower."

As fast as I can move with the pain I round the bed, headed to the private bathroom. "Delta," he barks, just as I close the door, leaving him alone with her. I ignore him, pressing my back against it, my eyes welling up with tears from the guilt . . . or the hormones. I'm not sure which at this point. I could be insane, but I know he won't hurt her. I feel it in my heart. With Kross there is no middle ground, no slow easement from one thing to another. It's all or nothing. I've known this since we started this relationship. I push. He requires the shove to do anything outside of his comfort zone. He never had anyone to teach him, so he doesn't learn that way. He learns by teaching himself in privacy without any spectators, so for fifteen minutes I'm going to give him time to bond with his daughter without judgment from anyone else.

I glance in the frosted mirror from the steam covering the bathroom, brushing through my long, wet hair, finally feeling just a tad bit back to normal. Thank God I'm out of that hospital gown and in my own pajamas. I set the brush on the counter and quickly brush my teeth, before slowly making my way back to the door. I take a deep breath as my hand grips the door handle, before finally opening it and taking a step out, preparing for his anger to hit the second I do.

It never comes.

I turn toward them, and with one glance my entire spirit is broken, my soul crushed, and my heart destroyed. My face becomes soaked in a matter of seconds. I slowly make my way around the bed, easing with each step forward, until I'm standing in front of him, in front of them. His tattooed hand seems bigger against her, but her tiny hand is wrapped around his index finger. As a lover of ink, the contrast of her creamy skin against his tattoos is beautiful. I don't know what to do or say. He grips the front neckline of his shirt with the opposite hand and wipes the inside down his face to rid of the evidence, but instead of letting go he keeps the fabric over his face.

"Kross . . . Don't hide from me. I'm the one person you don't have to hide from."

In a voice more raw than I've ever heard it, he says. "The devil doesn't cry."

I straddle his lap in the oversized hospital chair and grip his face in my hands, ignoring the pain between my legs, Emery between us. "That may be so, but a father does. There is nothing wrong with feeling something for someone so deep that it overwhelms you. It's completely normal."

"I feel something for you."

"Yes, and because of those feelings we created her. She's the beautiful parts of me, and the beautiful parts of you. That makes it a different kind of feeling than anything you feel for me. A new feeling."

A tear falls from his eye, hitting against the skin between my thumb and forefinger. "I don't remember it being like this."

"Me either, and it's okay. We don't have to have it together right now. Bringing a person into the world is scary and exciting. We can figure it out together, yeah?"

"And if I fail?"

"Then we try again. Even kings fail sometimes—the most powerful of all men."

"I'm protective of her."

"I'd be worried if you weren't."

"I love you, Delta. You make my goddamn heart ache."

I lean in, careful not to press against her, my lips an inch away from his. "I know the feeling. From the first time I saw you I knew you'd break down my walls. I've been trying to break down yours ever since."

He grabs the back of my head and kisses me in a way that leaves an imprint on the soul. A fire ignites and heats every corridor in my body. I pull away at the sound of her cry, wanting him in a way I've never wanted him before. "It's going to be a long six weeks," I whisper.

His eyes darken with hunger. "I'm not much of a rule follower. There are ways to bend them to my will."

That's it. I need to get out of this hospital before I make really bad decisions and jump his bones, consequences be damned . . .

Kross

Emery cries from the little rocking thing next to Delta's side of the bed. It looks like a cocoon or sling hanging from a metal frame. I keep saying that it can't be good for her spine but Delta swears up and down the reviews are good and if it wasn't safe it wouldn't be on the market. It's a fight I didn't win, even though I volunteered to move her crib in here. She claims if we do that we'll never get her out and it'll destroy our sex life and take away the intimacy of our relationship. I don't see how. Nothing could change that.

I roll over on top of Delta, holding myself off of her. I've been staring at the ceiling for about three hours, waiting and thinking since my feeding at 3AM. I offered to take the middle of the night feeding since I've always been up this time anyway, but this particular one has me on edge.

It's been two weeks since we came home from the hospital and there is one thing missing. It's something I should have done a long time ago. If I were being honest, I've considered it in my head for a while, trying to work out the pros and cons. All I seem to come up with are positives; however, the fear of the negatives should I not do it are what keeps replaying in my head, over and over, as if it's stuck on repeat.

I kiss her neck, my tongue tasting her skin. She pushes her head back and wraps her legs around me, her eyes still closed, giving me more room. I make my way to her jaw, but before I get there she's already pushing my briefs over my ass. "Kross, I need you."

"Still got four more weeks, baby."

She growls out, pulling me between her legs. "I don't care. I want you to do it. That's probably just a precaution."

Emery cries again. Her cries are so soft they're easy to tune out. I pull the lobe of her ear between my teeth. "Baby is up."

Her eyes finally open. "Okay."

I kiss her. "You change her and I'll get the bottle."

"You don't have to. It's my turn. You can sleep," she says, sleepily.

I smirk. "Been up. Was waiting on you. I'll get the bottle."

I move off of her so she can sit up. "You're in a good mood for it to be this early. What am I missing? You're hard and not getting laid.

I don't smell your death coffee. And there is a little person crying at the butt-crack of dawn. Are you possessed?" Her eyes widen with wakefulness. "I swear on all that is holy, if you're high I will fucking punch you. I may have chosen bottles over boobs because of the metal compromising my nipples but that is completely unfair."

I stand, pulling on a pair of cotton pants from the dresser. "It's a good thing your morning moodiness has always been a turn-on for me. I may not be getting laid, but I nut just fine with your lips wrapped around it. Secondly, coffee is an option for me, not a requirement. And I haven't been high in months. Lastly, if I pissed myself constantly and had to depend on someone to change me I'd throw a fit too. Don't blame her. Change her. I'll be back."

And with her sitting in the bed, gaping at me, I leave the room.

Detta

Emery cries out again, drawing my attention. I pick her up out of the Rock 'N Play, still tightly swaddled, cradling her in my arms. I kiss her forehead as I run my fingers through her headful of silky, black hair. I was a little shocked she had so much. I can put tiny bows in it already. "You are one powerful little person, Emery. You have Daddy wrapped around your finger. I'm a little jealous."

I stand and walk to her room, laying her down on the changing table to change her diaper. I pull the blanket open, instantly confused. "What are you wearing? Did you mess up your clothes?"

When she went to bed she was wearing a footed sleeper and now she's wearing a black, long sleeve onesie with the sleeve ends folded over her hands. It's one I've never seen before; the writing on the front crumpled some because she's so little. I unbutton the bottom and pull it down to stretch it out. "Oh . . . God."

I wipe the tears from my eyes as I read the vinyl for the fifth time: Mommy, will you marry Daddy?

I pick her up and snuggle her to my chest, before turning to go find Kross. I stop dead in my tracks when my eyes land on him. He's kneeling down on one knee, a ring box in his hands, open, with a one-of-a-kind ring nestled inside. "You do have me wrapped around your finger, Delta. The only woman that ever has. I know I'm a little late, but this is the only thing left to make you completely mine. You left me once. I hated every second you were gone. I'll do anything to make sure it doesn't happen again. You're already my girl, my roommate, my best friend, and the mother of my daughter, so I'm going to ask you . . . Will you be my wife?"

"Are you fucking serious?"

Tears are pouring down my face to the point that he's blurry.

He shines the smile that makes me weak at the knees—the panty dropper as I call it. "I'm fucking serious," he answers, and takes the ring from the box, before grabbing my left hand and sliding it just over the tip. "What's it going to be, baby? Yes or no. I'm not sure my heart can take the latter."

"Yes, I'll marry you! I thought you'd never ask."

He pushes the ring on my finger, sliding it into place. The band is black and consists of three large, round-cut diamonds in a single row, the middle twice the size of the ones flanking it. Each diamond is showcased in a V-shaped setting of small, round diamonds lightening the dark they're placed in. They're raised from the band, showing off all angles to catch the light. It's beautiful, but that's not even the part that has me crying all over again. Capping each end is a small skull in black to match the band, the back of the skull flush against the end diamond setting, the mouth facing another small patch of diamonds. It's perfect in every sense of the word. It's us. "Where did you get this?"

He stands, pulling Emery and me against his bare chest. "It's a Jeulia design I took to a jeweler and had custom made. In life and in death you're the only girl for me. Either side we stand on, I promise it'll be together. Forever will never be more literal for anyone than me. I love you. Both of you."

This man will never understand how beautiful he truly is. No one loves harder than the ones that fought through hatred and heartache to find it. I'm honored to call him mine. I'm lucky that he chose me. And if he'll have me, I'll never let him go. "I love you too. I really do."

THE END. FOR NOW.

What to expect next from Shadows in the Dark series:
Forever Marked (Kaston and Lux)
Love After War (Leads into a spin-off series for
the tattoo shop! Continue for chapter one!)

LOVE AFTER WAR

Delta

I stare at the neon tattoo sign on the brick building, hands clenched around the steering wheel of my Infinity, my eyes welling up with tears. Emery is screaming in her car seat in the back, most likely hungry. I should be at home since she hasn't had her vaccine shots yet, but I can't stand the sight of those walls anymore. They're closing in. I may very well go insane. I've been stuck at home since she was born, and I've never been a homebody. It seems like Kross is always gone, either at the shop or on a job. I feel alone in my own home, but I refuse to say anything. I won't be a nagging fiancé. I can't help but think he's probably gone no more than he's always been. The difference is—I feel trapped there while he can come and go freely.

Kross refuses to let me go anywhere, afraid something will happen to one of us. He plays it off that she'll get sick, but I know him well enough to pick up on his fear. It comes out when he's an extra-special asshole. I love him for it, but I hate him for it too. I miss this place. I miss working. I miss the guys. I miss Cassie, even though she comes to see us once a week. But most of all, I miss holding that tattoo gun. I miss seeing the look on the client's face when their dream became a reality. I miss knowing my artwork is walking around in the world. I miss working next to Kross, knowing I'm worthy of being there. I was just getting started in my career, only to have it taken from me. I love my daughter, but there is suitable childcare, if her father would deem someone good enough . . .

Kross told me I could stay home with our daughter permanently, that I should, hinting that's what he wanted, but I'm not meant to just sit at home and clean and bake pies and shit. I know there are women that would kill to be in my shoes, but I respect that some of us are meant to be tied to a household and some of us are meant to be career women. To top it off, my hormones are making me crazy. Scale wise, I weigh less than I did when I got pregnant, but my ass feels fat, my tits gained a permanent cup size, even not breastfeeding, and my stomach isn't as firm as it was after being stretched to house a person.

My mind is jumping to conclusions, making me hate myself. My six-week checkup was yesterday. I'm no longer bleeding, and I was cleared for sex by my doctor, yet my fiancé didn't even remember. I was expecting for him to come home after his delivery and lay it on me, but instead, he kissed me and our daughter, and then went to bed, only to be back up three hours later and leaving to come here. I cried the second he left.

Every man remembers the date in which he's free to let his dick roam in a woman's wet wonderland when going without, unless he's already getting it somewhere else. Is Kross a typical man where sex is concerned? Well, no, and I know a lot of it stems from his childhood. He could go without sex longer than I could. And when he wants it, there is always a little force and harshness involved. That's all he's ever known. But look at him. God, he's hot. He's got that dark mystery thing down to an art that makes girls want to stand in front of him naked and beg for it.

I need to know he still wants me the way he did before my body was altered by a tiny human. I've been a mother for six weeks. I've been engaged a little less. It's always going to be in the back of my mind that he proposed after he knocked me up. I can't help it. I'm a woman, and no matter how much I tell myself that I walked away and he fought for me, I need him to show it more than he tells me. I understand now why you're supposed to be married before you bring kids into it. It's a mindfuck in itself.

Emery's cry gets louder, reminding me that she's depending on me. I pull down the visor and check my hair and makeup in the mirror, making sure it's exactly how it was when I left the house. After I stopped crying, I decided that I'm responsible for the outcome of my life. No one else. I got up, showered, and took extra time getting ready while she napped. I can't let my feelings fester, which brings me to the here and now.

I kill the engine and walk to the back door, sliding on the seat beside her car seat base. Her eyes are closed, and her face is soaked, her mouth wide and her voice loud, lungs backing that cry. "Hey, little girl," I say, grabbing her pacifier from between her legs to put it in her mouth. "You're not going to get anywhere with your daddy's attitude." I have to shake it on her tongue a few times for her to realize it's there. She finally closes her mouth around the nipple and starts to suckle, eyeballing me like I should know I'm her bitch. Yep, definitely Kross' kid.

I take a deep breath, already unbuckling the straps to get her out, and then lift her tiny body out and bring her to my chest, both arms locked around her. I rub my lips over her silky black hair, my heart so full it could burst, making me feel guilty that I want to come back to work. "What am I going to do with you?"

Scooting to the edge of the leather seat, I grab the black backpack covered in skulls with her initials monogrammed in pink on the front off the floorboard, pulling the strap on one shoulder before replacing my arm across her back and standing from the car. Her cheek is pressed against my chest, our warmth passing through each other. I shut the door. With one button on the keyless entry I lock the car, and then make my way to the glass door of *Inked aKross the Skin*. A customer walks out of the door just as I approach, holding it open for me. "Thank you," I say, passing through, a ping of disappointment occurring that he didn't recognize me as one of the artists.

"Bring me that baby!" Cassie squeals, holding her arms out in front of her with her fingers waving back and forth, showing her excitement. "Kross didn't tell me you were coming by today."

"It's a surprise," I say, handing her Emery. Cassie adjusts Emery on her chest and sits back in her seat, already turning side to side in her rolling chair to comfort her. For someone that doesn't have kids I've always noticed how much of a natural she is with Emery. She's better at it than me.

Emery whimpers, finally deciding the pacifier isn't giving her any formula. "Bottle?"

I open the diaper bag and hand her a pre-made bottle, minus the top. Within seconds she has Emery cradled in her arms and the bottle in her mouth, all without her head bobbing around like a bobble head. "Were you one of those girls that babysat at a young age?"

She glances up at me, a half-smile already in place. "I was sixteen when my brother was born."

"Oh, well at least I feel better now. I think to myself, I'm doing pretty damn good at this whole mom thing, and then I see you with her and I can't help but feel inadequate. I was prepared to curse you if you were a natural born baby whisperer. I still want to pull my hair out at two a.m. feedings and I've had weeks to adjust."

She smiles at me—that warm Cassie smile that makes you wonder where in the hell Kross found a girl like her to be a receptionist. Always happy and welcoming. Perfect for the job. But also too good for it. "Nope. I had lots of practice. You'll get there, Mama. By the darling of darkness' chunky cheeks, I'd say you're doing a fine job so far."

Guilt consumes my heart again. I feel that I fall short where motherhood is concerned. "Can I bribe you to babysit for a little while?"

Her brow arches. "Like you had to ask. Shoo. It's Auntie Cassie's time."

"He in the studio?"

Her mouth tilts. "He is right now, but if he sees you he may not be for long. Lookin' good to have just spit out this cute munchkin, lil' mama."

That's what I'm hoping for . . .

I smile. Sometimes a compliment is more valuable than a million dollars. I spin on my heels, already trekking across the floor toward the stairs. I can do this. I got him when he wasn't mine. I shouldn't have any problem now that he is . . . I hope.

Kross

The studio door opens halfway through Vinny's neck piece, not drawing my attention. That damn door doesn't stay closed for long as busy as we've been. Then Remington whistles, causing all of the buzzing in the room to cease. "Damn, Delta."

I glance up at the sound of her name, already wanting to drive a screwdriver through his retinas for looking at her, my eyes locking with hers. One thought registers. "Where's my daughter?"

"With Cassie. I need to talk to you."

I make the mistake of dropping my eyes. Her nipples are straining against her tight shirt, the metal balls of her nipple rings noticeable, meaning she's wearing a thin bra. She knows better than to come in the lion's den looking like a raw steak. It stays cold up here to keep down bacteria with open skin and needles. I can't handle germs. Last thing I need is fucking staph coating every surface, or worse.

My eyes veer to way too much visible thigh. Her shorts are barely covering her ass. I want to kill fewer people when she's not here. Yet I can watch her when she is. It's a fucking vicious cycle I can't seem to break. My dick is straining against my jeans like her presence alone commands it to rise. I'll never tell her how much power she really holds over me. And it's been too fucking long since I've been inside her. My thoughts are dark. My cravings are volatile. My need is high. Her body isn't ready for the hostile behavior I know is coming. I'm almost afraid to fuck her. So I haven't.

I have too much bad blood running through my veins. I watched my father do despicable things to my mother's body at a vulnerable age. I lived through a woman raping me over and over. For years I used sex as a release, only when I was on the verge of detonating. I controlled my own body no different than I did a woman's. There is nothing sensual mapped in my DNA. I like sex fast, hard, and borderline abusive. The appeal to take it without asking is far too strong. The thought of controlling her like a puppet makes me rock hard.

But she's no longer a stripper. She's no longer my whore. She's not the sexy troubled girl that walked in my shop and needed me for a job, or the girl I knocked up, despite me trying to blame it on her. She's not a cheap slut I demanded to abort my fuckup. She's my fiancé. I love her. The second I can con someone into filing a marriage license without all that other ridiculous shit she'll be my wife. She gave me my daughter. I watched her do it. There is no way she's healed enough for how hard I want to abuse her sweet pussy. I don't give a damn what any person holding a medical license says. She's the mother of my child. She deserves something I don't know how to give her. She needs husband sex. And until I can figure out what that is, I'll make myself wait. She walked away from me once. She won't do it again. I'll bury her in a box first.

I force my eyes back to hers, and then break contact to reload the gun. "I'm busy. What is it?"

Tattoo guns start up again, like music to my ears. I go back to Vinny's tattoo. "It's not something I can talk about here," she says.

"I'll be done in a few hours. It'll have to wait."

"It can't. It's important."

I don't know why in the fuck we're having a personal conversation in front of clients. She knows that's not allowed. "I'm in the middle of a session, Delta. You know Vinny comes from Detroit."

"Goddammit, Kross, I need you to fuck me," she shouts, an edge to her tone, drawing everyone's attention in the room. The sound of silence. I can hear every breath. I freeze, staring at the half-inked tattoo, watching his pulse as his heart pumps blood through his artery, counting, and thinking of how easy it'd be to silence that too. Every vile of blood in my body is at a standstill, rage consuming me. Then her voice changes, cooling me down like someone throwing a cooler of ice-cold water on an open fire. I'd know that sound anywhere. She's crying. "I've been stuck at home for what seems like forever, while the world around me keeps turning as if no one knows I'm gone. I'm covered in smelly spit-up. All I do anymore is change diapers and make bottles. My body doesn't look like it did before. I've probably forgotten how to hold a tattoo gun. When the delivery boy brings takeout at dinner is the only adult conversation I get. We haven't had sex since before I gave birth. Yesterday I was given the go-ahead and you went to sleep. I need you to fuck me. Just break the damn ice. Otherwise, you're fucking someone else."

What?

I look up at her beautiful, wet face, blinking, forgetting that every goddamn person in this room has a front row seat to my personal life, trying to process what she just said. Fucking someone else? She should know better. Then I remember that night about a year ago, right after I had fucked her for the first time. We went a couple weeks without it, which was more than normal for me, but she got upset, and somehow it came up that she needed me to fuck her to know that I was interested.

Vinny cuts in before I can formulate an answer. "Bruh, you better take care of that. Or I will. I can wait."

"I'll meet you in my office."

She swipes underneath her heavily lined eyes and disappears down the stairs, slamming the door shut behind her. I stare at it, trying to figure out how we got here. We haven't had a fight since the night she told me Emery was a girl, because I was staking out my mom's killer, and sperm donor—had been for a while. I've been working my ass off to keep my mind off of that. I can't look at her without thinking about fucking her. As far as her body goes—it looks better now than it did before. I've never been interested in shoving my cock in a girl's ass till recently. I don't know if it all really bounced back better or if it's because I know it was my kid's lifeline for almost a year. "You don't have to understand them to make them happy," Vinny says. "Your girl wants you to lay it on her, you don't ask questions. If you won't, there is always a guy that will."

"Take a smoke break. I'll be back. This tattoo is on me." I lay my tattoo gun down and stand, jerking my black, latex gloves off my hands, my stool rolling backward. And then I walk to the door and stop, the room still silent when it should be thundering with the buzzing of needles penetrating skin and casual conversation. "This shit ever leaves this room I have a bullet with your name on it."

The buzzing starts up again, and voices mixing fills the room. I rip open the door, inflicting stress on the hinges, knowing my private life will remain private. My reputation of keeping my promises is well earned. Everyone in a chair today is male, and a regular. Thank God. Now, I'm about to take care of my other problem, and hers. Husband sex is for pussies. Like the asshole that I am, I'm about to tear that shit up. It's time to remind her what got her pregnant in the first place.

Detta

I stare at the various enlarged photos of tattoos he's done on the wall behind his desk, crying hysterically. My goal was to pull him aside and just kind of start kissing him. I never meant to scream that out. To air out all my dirty laundry—our dirty laundry. He kept brushing me off, making me wait, and I snapped. I've been alone too long, and he has a way of drawing my worst out of me. He's going to be pissed. His biggest rule is no personal shit in the studio with clients, me included. He's never coddled me in front of the guys. I'm expected to follow the same rules. I get the same consequences if I break them.

The door opens and closes, causing my heart to race. Fuck. My shoulders draw closer to my ears, every muscle tensing. Waiting. Anticipating. The air shifts around me, and I may not can hear his footsteps, but I can feel him behind me, just like that day of the interview . . . "I'm sorry."

"You think I'd fuck another woman?"

So Kross-like. Straight to the point. "Yes. No. I don't know. You didn't even try . . . My body—"

"Looks better."

I start to cry again, feeling more foolish with every minute that passes. "I miss you. I miss us."

"I haven't gone anywhere."

This is not coming out how I wanted it to. Maybe I just need to go home and calm down and try this again when the embarrassment has dissolved. "Never mind," I say, trying to dodge around him.

His hand clamps around the front of my neck like a vise, his grip stern, showing his authority, before drawing me back to his front. I close my eyes when the bulge in the front of his jeans presses against my ass. "You had shit to say. Say it."

"We haven't had sex in two months, considering you wouldn't fuck me the last two weeks of my pregnancy, and the day I'm clear you didn't even seem fazed. You forgot. I even reminded you about my appointment, so you didn't lose your shit when you checked my location."

"No, I didn't."

"Have you even thought about it?"

"Every fucking moment I'm conscious."

"Then why didn't you?"

He slams my body against the wall, the side of my face striking against the glass of the frame as his hand rotates from the front of my neck to the back, not loosening in the least. His lips scrape against my skin on the path toward my ear. "Everything I represent is carnal, raw. You're the girl I blew my load in. Whether I ever admitted it aloud or not, I chose you to have my kid. To be my wife. You're my ride or die bitch. It's no secret that I'll kill you before I let you go. I'll bury bodies that come between us. I'll love you 'til the end. Thought you deserved something different to show you what I can't tell you. I don't know how to love you slow. To fuck you soft. To give you husband sex. Make you feel shit. I was punishing myself 'til I figured it out."

I think I just fell in love with him all over again. Kross' mind is vastly different from anyone I've ever known. The way he thinks, processes, understands. There will never be another like him. There will never be another man that can make a threat of killing his fiancé romantic. He's already been my savior. Proven his love to me. Made forever appealing. "Why didn't you just talk to me?"

"Talking is overrated."

"It solves problems. If that's what husband sex is, I don't want husband sex," I whisper, as his hand snakes under my shirt, quickly descending to the waistband of my shorts where it roughly dips underneath. He drives his boot against the inside of my foot, forcing my legs apart. My knees buckle when his callused finger presses into my slit, already rubbing my clit. My hands fist around the denim of his jeans at the same time his short nails dig into the skin of my neck, holding me up with a tight grip. It hurts, but I don't want him to let go.

Every breath I take creates a fog against the frame glass. I close my eyes, trying to absorb the shockwaves rolling through my body with each stroke he makes. I missed him touching me. "Then what do you want?"

"I want Kross sex. I want the pain mixed with the pleasure. I want you to abuse my body right before you worship it—the only way you know how. I want the no filter asshole that comes forth right before the man that tells me he'll love me 'til the end."

The second I start to come he cups his hand over my mound and drives two fingers inside of me so hard that it forces me on my toes, drawing a loud, embarrassing moan out of me before I can stop it. I grip one hand around his thick, corded ink-covered forearm that's running down my belly, feeling every tendon drawing up and releasing as he finger-fucks me in a stabbing motion, stretching me and forcing my body to constrict at the same time. "Let it out, baby. You announced what you wanted to the whole fucking studio, they're going to hear you too."

Right before my orgasm fades, he jerks me backward by both hold points on my body and shuffles us around until I'm pressed against his desk, his hands already shoving my shirt up my stomach. Reflexively, I suck in as his hand passes over the softer skin that was stretched over my baby less than two months ago. He removes my shirt, tossing it down. "Stop. Why the fuck are you suddenly worried about your body? You weren't that worried about it when I wanted to murder every guy that drooled over you when it was barely covered." He bites against my ear.

"It's a little hard not to be paranoid next to yours. You don't have an ounce of fat. Your skin is tight against your abs. Mine changed. Yours didn't." My bra falls down my arms with little effort on his part. His tattooed hands come around my waist, quickly undoing my shorts before shoving them to the floor, leaving me naked.

I try to lean forward over the desk, hoping he actually chooses right now to just give it to me from behind and not call me out on my insecurities. I've never been worried about my body. On the contrary, actually. I always loved showing it off. It was more for the tattoo showcasing than my figure itself. At this moment, I just feel awkward in my own skin. I'm skinny, but soft. You don't think much about your firm, toned body until you can't fall back on it anymore.

I barely have time to register his belt buckle jingling before he's slamming into me, shoving me forward across the glossy wood. A satiated groan falls from my lips with the fullness at my core. Fuck, I've missed this. Never loved a man's cock like I love his. I grip the farthest edge of the desk, waiting for it like a student anticipating a wooden paddle, but instead of feeding into my need, he grips my long, black, wand-curled hair in his fist and pulls me back, a burning sensation occurring at my roots, causing an unexpected yell.

My shoulder blades meet a bare, sculpted torso, warm to the touch, and his arm stretches across my front from waist to the opposite shoulder like the strap of a bag. The second he releases my hair, his rough hand clenches the back of my thigh, hoisting my leg up until the back of my knee is hooked in the bend of his arm, forcing my body to feel every thick lengthy inch. "Guess I'll have to show you how much I appreciate the new version then," he says, and then pounds into me relentlessly, forcing my body to comply, reminding me how much I love his strength and size.

His hard body strikes against mine over and over, not caring that he's fucking me so deep I can feel him in my abdomen. My hand combs through his hair and I pull, pushing up on the tips of my toes, straining my calf, trying to close the gap in our height to minimize the pain. I'm stretched to the max. Filled to the brim. I pull away. It makes him drive harder, faster, abusing my body to no avail. I clench around him, my muscles trying to absorb some of the shock he's causing, and then another orgasm builds from him hitting the spot just right. "Jesus Christ," he seethes, before shoving me down on the desk so far up my feet won't touch the floor.

My back arches. His front presses firmer against my back, leaving virtually no space between us. Every new thrust comes before he completely recoils, not giving me time to recover. My eyes are closed. My mouth is agape. I can't concentrate. I have no idea if I'm screaming or cussing or panting. All I know is that it feels better than anything I can describe and I'm going to have bruises between my thighs. Then he grabs my chin and forces my head to turn so hard I'm positive a nerve was pinched in the process, a shooting pain spreading through my neck.

As his lips consume mine and his fingers dig into my ass cheek, he stills, spilling his cum inside of me. Seconds later, he pulls out, flipping me over as if I weigh nothing, and then comes back over me, his beautiful, ink-covered body making my heart pound. His lips close around my nipple. He sucks, before drawing back, the barbell of my nipple ring between his teeth. I run my fingers through the lengthy top of his hair, making a mess of it as he continues to give my breasts attention. He never leaves them out. "I love you, Kross."

Without saying a word, he grips the backs of my thighs and pushes them back, kissing his way down my stomach, spending extra time on each of the few stretch marks that surround my belly button, before ending between my lips, his tongue flicking and his mouth sucking. "Oh, fuck. You haven't done that in so long."

I buck against his mouth, grinding and writhing under his hold, already sensitive from earlier. He doesn't give me room to move until he demands for me to come again. When he comes back up, he stops at my stomach, his forehead pressed against my diaphragm. I don't know what he's doing. Then he kisses my stomach in the same place he used to randomly kiss it when I was pregnant. "Kross."

"This gave her life. It protected her even from a bastard like me. It's beautiful." My brows draw in, confused, my eyes already welling up with tears.

I tug on his hair until he finally looks at me, something in his eyes I don't understand. "What do you mean?"

"Had you listened to me, she wouldn't be here. Your body kept her safe. Stop worrying about imperfections only you see. This is mine. Only mine."

A tear streaks down my face. "Come here. Please."

He complies, surprisingly. "Talk to me. Tell me what's in your head."

"One day she will know I didn't want her. I want her. I'll spend the rest of her life making it up to her, and you."

I sit up, grabbing his face in my hands. His jeans are so low you can still see the base of his dick, as if he just kind of pulled them up enough to partially cover himself. I kiss him. "You beautiful asshole. She'll never know. She will never know. I will never tell her. I forgive you. Now forgive yourself."

He blinks at me, over and over, silent. I'm not sure what to make of it. Kross is always in his head, thinking and putting things together. He's impossible to read. You become dependent on his lack of filter to know what's going on inside, because otherwise, he's blank space. "Go get an application for a fucking marriage license. I'll sign it."

I laugh through my tears, pulling his big body against mine.

"Only if you let me come back to work."

He grumbles, just like I knew he would. He knew this was coming. "Part time."

I sigh. "Can I argue terms?"

"No."

I roll my eyes. "Fine. What else?"

He stands, grabbing his shirt and putting it back on, fiancé Kross gone and business Kross now in place. "I have to be present for childcare interviews. I will do a fucking background check. I will have hidden cameras. Until we find someone good enough, Cassie can watch her when you're here. I'll double her pay."

"No offense, but you're scary in interviews. You're an asshole of a boss too. You'll send any prospects running."

"Then they don't need to be responsible for my daughter. If they can deal with me, they deserve the job." Palms to the desk, my head falls back. I sigh, listening to his belt as he buckles it. He's a pain in my ass most days, but I wouldn't survive without him. His face comes over me, but upside down from mine. He kisses me, before tossing soft cotton at me—my shirt. "I'll be home by eight. If you're going to want food, better eat before."

I smirk. "Are you going to lock me up and make me your sex slave? You're rarely home that early."

"Something like that." He looks at me for a minute. "I'll make some changes. I would never fuck another woman. You fuck another man there will be one less dick in the world. I will give you what you need."

My heart plummets to my stomach. I hop off the table, quickly pulling my shirt on, forgoing the bra. It's so thin it doesn't make a difference anyway. Wrapping my arms around his waist, I look up at him, straining with the height difference. "I'm yours. Only yours." He picks me up, minimizing the distance between us. My legs wrap around his waist, my arms around his neck, and I press my forehead to his. "And you're all mine. I was letting my thoughts run away. I'm sorry."

He walks me toward the wall, pressing my back against it. "I meant what I said. Go get the application. I want it done."

I smile. "Ever the romantic one. What if I want a wedding?"

"You don't. If you did I wouldn't have asked you to marry me. Shit's not happening. I don't like people. Name a place you want to go and I'll take—" I shut him up with my mouth, calming him down. A wedding never even crossed my mind. I think I just assumed we'd be engaged forever and that would be good enough for me. I know he doesn't like people. I don't really like many people either. That's why we're one and the same.

He pulls back. "I gotta get to work."

I slide down his body, not wanting to leave. "I know."

"You owe me enough sex to cover that tattoo."

I laugh, scurrying to find my shorts, quickly pulling them on and adjusting them into place. He waits for me, like the asshole-ish gentleman that he is. "Like when I owed you that blowjob the last time I had an outburst where you're concerned? At this rate I'll be indebted to you sexually forever."

"That's what I'm counting on," he says, opening the door as soon as I come up behind him, guiding me out before he follows. He plants a quick kiss on my lips. "I'll call you later."

When we make it into the lobby, Remington is standing at the counter, a toothpick between his lips and a grin too massive to be excited about work on his face. Cassie's face is blood red, holding a sleeping Emery. "Sex is in the air," he says, and then acts like he's taking a whiff.

I clamp my mouth shut, trying not to make the mistake of laughing. Remington loves pissing Kross off, making him uncomfortable, and though he'd never admit it, I think Kross respects him more for it. He did promote him to shop manager, after all. I may be holding back the laugh, but the guilty smile is spread wide. I can feel it. Kross makes his way to the studio door, jerking it open. "Not a fucking word!" he shouts, and then slams the door shut behind him, already heading up the stairs.

Cassie looks at the door, silent for a few seconds, and then turns back toward me when the other door slams shut upstairs. "I don't think you realized how loud that was. I have to ask, is he as beastly in the sack as he is around here?"

One simple reply is all it takes for Kross to make sense. "What you see is what you get."

Remington glances at her from his propped position on the counter, and by the look in his eyes, I know something is coming. "I bet I can do it better. And I won't get you pregnant."

Cassie rolls her eyes, the laugh tumbling out before the words. "Not happening, slut."

God it feels good to be back. It's batshit crazy around here, but it's a crazy I miss desperately when it's gone . . .

ALSO BY CHARISSE SPIERS

Do I have any music lovers here? Do you want access to my "Love and War" Spotify playlist? Here's the link below (click playlist) . . .

Love and War Playlist

P.S. I feel I should explain my book playlists first before you go "what? 130 something songs." lol. Mine are not traditional book playlists at 12 or so songs. These are my "writing playlists" so the more songs the better since I listen as I write. When I hear a song, if a certain couple starts playing out scenes in my head, that song goes onto their playlist. Not EVERY word of EVERY song will be accurate to the plot, but the feel, the emotions behind the song, the mood, the lyrics, and the vibe in general—all that goes into the development of my stories, so if you want to listen, there it is. Free accounts can listen in shuffle mode with the occasional commercial.

xoxo,

Charisse

If you liked the men of *Inked aKross the Skin,* there will be a spin-off series with Kross, Delta, their life in tattoo, and the characters in the shop (at some point). I'm already getting requests for Johnny's book, Wesson's, and Remington's. The stories are talking, if I can just find the time to write them.

A NOTE FROM THE AUTHOR

Thank you so much for reading Love and War! I hope you enjoyed their story. Kross and Delta are very special to me. I know for a lot of you, the wait for them was long. I hope it was worth every month you had to wait. If you enjoyed their story, please consider leaving a review on the retailer of your choice.

If you are following the Shadows in the Dark series, next up is Forever Marked, the continuation of Kaston and Lux, so if you did not read Marked prior to reading Love and War, go read it for FREE to get ready for their follow up.

Other characters, like Chevy (he has not been forgotten), will follow. Also, at some point, there will be a spin-off series of Inked aKross the Skin, following the characters in shop like Remington, Wesson, and possibly more.

As always, I will keep what project I'm working on up to date on social media. Thank you for the continued support.

I love all of my readers dearly.

XOXO,

Charisse

ACKNOWLEDGMENTS

As I embark on my fourth year publishing anniversary, I want to say how truly blessed I am to be a part of this community. I don't always frequent social media if you're a loyal follower, because I use it as a business platform and not a personal tool, but I am there. I do get on and check notifications, answer messages, comments, and tags as long as I see it. I participate as time allows. Usually Instagram is where I post the most. Between a full time job, being a wife, a mother, and trying to give time to my writing life and attention to my characters, sometimes it's not often.

This community has pulled me through some dark times, and it gave me a life I never even dreamed of. That is why my biography will always be in first person, giving you a small personal look into what makes me, me, and to show how much books impacted my life, not only as an author, but first a reader. I still sit on the other side of books, allowing myself to get lost in the characters as merely a reader, letting all the feels consume me as I experience someone else's story. It is something I'll never give up completely, no matter how busy I become with my own books.

Writing, on the other hand, is also something I need. It's an outlet for me. Did I sit as I child and envision myself as being a writer like so many did—no. But now that I'm here, I think, how did I ever get along without it? In that sense it's like being a mother. You don't know what you're missing until it becomes a part of you, and then, you know you can't live without it. Fiction is a happy place for me. The stories are my literary babies—something I pour my heart and soul into—and the reader gives them the magic to come to life through reading, loving, recommending, making teasers and leaving reviews.

If you're still reading, I want to thank the readers for continuing to support my writing. I know I don't always write in the order you may want, but know that every book will come out when it's supposed to. It has not been forgotten, not even Fate series. For me, the characters choose who is written next, and some of them are stronger than others. The ones that follow on social media do not go unnoticed. Your comments make me smile. Even the readers that remain publicly silent, but continue to purchase book after book, thank you. You all make the hard work worthwhile and keep the stories flowing. You guys are my motivation to continue day after day, year after year.

Thank you to my cover designer, Clarise Tan with CT Cover Creations, on such a beautiful cover. You, girl, are my Rockstar. Every design scheme in my head you execute better than I imagined.

Thank you to Darren Birks with Darren Birks photography for a kickass Delta, also known as Isabella "Bella" Frayne, and to Golden Czermak with Furious Fotog for the only Kross that ever fit, Andrew England. Both of these photographers put in so much time and effort to find and bring us authors models that make our characters that much more real. If you visit their website or social media pages, give them a shout out for their awesome hard work and tell them I sent you.

If you would like to be the first to know about my releases, giveaways, or excerpts, you are welcome to sign up for my newsletter. I promise I won't spam your inbox.

Elizabeth Thiele, my assistant, thank you for all the hard work you put in year after year that we've been together, even having a family of your own. Had you not come to me all those years ago after reading one of my books, I would have missed out on a beautiful friendship. I hope you will be there alongside me for many years to come.

Thank you to my beta readers; those I gladly call friends—Tammy Huckabee, Susan Walker, and Innergoddess booklover (for her privacy)

Last but not least, thank you to one of my very best friends, Nancy Henderson, writing under N. E. Henderson—my partner in crime, author buddy, signing co-author, print formatter and editor. Not only are you my best friend day in and day out, but also the person that helps me make my books better, my personal motivator, and the only one that truly understands what it's like to have characters screaming stories at you. We talk fiction as if they're real, for hours on end. I don't know what it'd be like to go a day without talking to you. You, and your never-ending love for Kross is probably why he's here now. If you haven't read her books, check them out. I know, personally, that you'll love them too. Visit her website here

Here's a toast to another year. I love you all.

XOXO,

Charisse

ABOUT THE AUTHOR

I found books when I was going through a hard time in life. They became my means of escape when things got bad. I realized quickly how much I loved to take a backseat to someone else's life and watch the journey unfold. That began my journey with books in November of 2012. I constantly had a book open on my Kindle app. Never in a million years would I have imagined myself as a writer, because I never thought I was creative enough. I'm living proof that things will fall into place when they're meant to be. People will make their way into our lives when we don't expect it, setting the path for what we are meant to do. Never give up on people. Never stop taking a chance on others. Someone took a chance on trusting me with her work when she didn't know me from a stranger on the street and gave me the opportunity of a lifetime as our relationship progressed, which led me to editing and writing as well. This is my dream I never knew I had. As soon as I sat down and gave writing a shot, it was like the floodgates opened. Now, I am lost in a world of fiction in my head, new characters constantly screaming for their stories to be told. Continue to dream and to go for them. No one ever found happiness by sitting on the sidelines. Sometimes we have to take risks and put ourselves out there. Thank you for all of your support, and may there be many books to come. XOXO- C

Stay up to date on release info
www.charissespiers.com
charissespiersbooks@gmail.com

Printed in Great Britain
by Amazon

41762804R10136